well-behaved woman coming undone

Debby Monk

Deborah Monk

Hudson, NH

well-behaved woman coming undone
by
Deborah Monk

ISBN: 978-1-7323384-1-8

Cover Design:
Melissa Luella, melissaluella.com

Interior Design:
Pamela Marin-Kingsley, pammarin-kingsley.com

Published by:

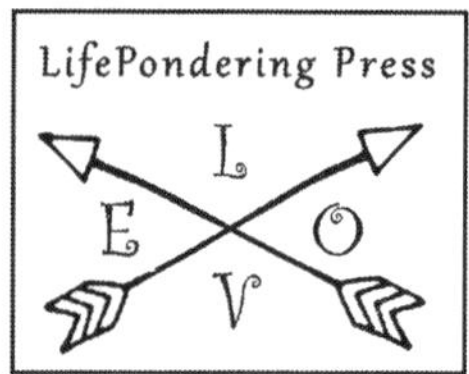

Hudson, New Hampshire
website: deborahmonk.com
Contact: deb@deborahmonk.com

For Sophie,
Watching you spread your wings,
inspires me to do the same.

"An invisible red thread connects those destined to meet,
regardless of time, place or circumstance.
The thread may stretch or tangle,
but never break."
-Ancient Chinese Proverb

Chapter One

Jodi

Of all the things I had hoped to do on my fortieth birthday, sitting on the toilet staring at a stick I peed on wasn't one of them.

I keep a stash of home pregnancy tests under the sink in my bathroom. Through most of my thirties, I was trying to get pregnant. Anyone who has had trouble getting pregnant knows the cycle. The week before your period, time slows down and you run to the bathroom every twenty minutes. Every second you get by without bleeding makes you hold your breath as your hopes start to rise. The minute your period is late, you dive under the sink for a pregnancy test, hoping it will be the last one you need. And when it shows negative, you're convinced that it doesn't mean anything because everyone knows it takes time for the hormones to show up in your urine.

When I turned thirty-eight, they found pre-cancerous cells in my uterus. My doctor did a procedure, doubled up on my Pap smears, and I've been fine ever since. Although she didn't say it would interfere with having another child, I had accepted it wasn't going to happen.

I felt guilty that my daughter wouldn't have a sibling,

guilty that my daughter's children wouldn't have cousins, guilty for the little boy in heaven who I know wanted me to be his mother, but what can I say...I tried.

So you can imagine my surprise this morning when I mentioned my early menopause on the phone to my best friend Gwen.

"How do you know you're going into early menopause?" she asked.

"Because I haven't had my period in three months. And I'm moody as hell. And horny! And let me tell you, moody and horny don't go well together. The other day I was so hot and bothered when Bob came home that I told him not to speak, to just get his butt up into the bedroom. You know what he did?"

"Ran upstairs?"

"No. He talked. And the sound of his voice annoyed me so much I couldn't have sex."

She laughed. "What did he have to say that couldn't wait?"

"You don't think I listened, do you? Anyway, I couldn't hear him over the singing."

"What singing?"

"I read somewhere that one of the signs of menopause is ringing in the ears. I don't hear ringing. I hear singing."

"Singing?"

"Doris Day is singing, 'Que Sera Sera' in my head twenty-four hours a day. You know—"When I was just a little girl, I asked my mother what will I be? Will I be pretty, will I be rich, here's what she said to me...."

"Maybe you're pregnant," she interrupted.

"Those aren't the words." I said, starting over. "Will I be pretty, will I be—"

"Pregnant," she said again. "Maybe you're pregnant."

"But I'm forty. Today." I reminded her. Like somehow that made a difference.

"Forty is young for menopause," she said. "It's just as possible you're—"

"But isn't forty too old to be pregnant?" If it's too young for menopause, and too old to be pregnant, what is forty good for?

I dropped in my chair in the kitchen. Would starting over with a new baby magically weave together my loose ends? Or would a baby grab onto my loose thread and unravel me completely?

Only five seconds until I can look at my urine soaked crystal ball to find out if I'm pregnant and that's when I hear a voice that sounds like Eartha Kitt echoing inside my chest. "I don't want to be."

"Don't want to be what?" I ask. I know it's a dumb question, that the answer seems obvious, but it wouldn't be so obvious if you started hearing, no, correct that, if you started feeling a voice that sounds suspiciously like Eartha Kitt purring inside your chest.

"I," she says slowly as if speaking slowly is going to help me understand. "Don't...want...to...be."

I interrupt before she can finish her sentence. "I've wanted another baby since Sofia was born."

"And for the first eight years or so, I was right there with you," she purrs.

Apparently, I am being haunted by Eartha Kitt, the singer that died a while back. I think she was the original Catwoman. But why is she talking inside my chest?

"Aren't you going to look?"

I pull the shower curtain back. Maybe Eartha is in my tub.

"Not for me," she says. "At the test."

Right. I pick the test up by the end, like I am planning to shake it like a thermometer if I don't like the results.

Not pregnant.

I drop my head on the side of the sink. Thank God.

"Thank heavens," Eartha sings, "for little girls."

I drop the test into the wastebasket. "Stop singing. It was negative. We're not pregnant." Even though I think I'm relieved, I feel tears lodged in the back of my throat.

"You know a negative at-home-test doesn't mean you're not pregnant. Remember Sofia?"

When I was pregnant with Sofia, I got a negative result on December second. And December fourth. And December sixth. The test instructions said the hormones double every forty-eight hours so I made myself wait an extra day. On December 9, I got a positive test. And nine months later, I got my baby.

"Speaking of Sofia," Eartha says, "isn't it time to pick her up from high school?"

Chapter Two

Jodi

The double doors open and spit out a jumble of adolescent human beings, hundreds of gangly limbs full of potential. I recognize my child even before I can distinguish her features. To the normal eye, she is just another teenage girl with dirty blonde hair dressed like every other kid in her blue jeans and sweatshirt. To me, she is the beginning and the end.

For a second, time shifts and I am sitting in the kindergarten parking lot. My little Sofia would come out of the school and her eyes would dart around looking for me, lighting up when she saw me. The teacher would have to hold her hand so she wouldn't run over to me. Back when nothing else mattered but me. Back when the word "Mom" overflowed with the purest love I've ever known.

Now I feel her eagle eyes pin me down like a frog in biology class. God forbid I am not here the minute she comes out of the building. As soon as she sees me, though, she forgets about me. As long as I am where she needs me to be, doing what she wants, I am invisible.

She is sandwiched between two friends and they're talking as if they haven't seen each other in years. Then she pulls out her phone, looks at the screen, and stops and shows it to her friends.

I wonder what she would say if I texted her, "I might be pregnant. You're going to have a baby brother or sister." Would she notice me then?

"How was your day?" I ask when she opens the door and slouches in the passenger seat.

"Fine," she mumbles.

If there was an award for being able to combine disdain and dismissal into one word, we'd need a bigger house for all her trophies.

Her phone buzzes, indicating she has a text. She reads it quickly. "Mom, can you drop me off at Sara's?"

"What about homework?" I ask, hating that I am reduced to the nagging mother script.

"I don't have any."

Sure. A sophomore in high school and she doesn't have any homework? "Fine," I mumble back. I want to put this stranger in a choke hold until she spits up my daughter, the one who loves me, adores me, thinks I can do no wrong. Then I'd leave this carcass of the obnoxious one on the side of the road. She obviously doesn't need a mother.

Maybe that's what scares me most—what if the one who doesn't need me is still in charge in a year when she can drive off and never look back?

I drive her to her friend's house in silence, missing the old her who loved the old me.

I had thought I might get a massage today, in honor of my birthday. Instead, I am sitting in my gynecologist's waiting room, the clipboard with the same medical form I have filled out on every other visit resting on my lap.

Forty.

Middle-aged.

Halfway through life.

I've read that for some people middle age is a time of reflection. A time of reevaluating their priorities. A second chance for something new.

If you were to ask me to describe my middle age, I would say middle age is exhaustion, rolled in frustration, toasted with tired, battered in—

"Mrs. Devlin? Are you finished with your form?"

I look up at the receptionist. Of course I wasn't. I pick the clipboard up off my lap and start filling in the blanks. "Just one more minute," I say,

> Name: Jodi Devlin. *Easy*
> Age: Forty. *Happy Birthday to me. Today's surprise...I might be pregnant with a change of life baby.*
> Weight: One hundred and sixty pounds. *Outright lie—I'm past one hundred and seventy but I won't admit that in writing.*
> Mother: Deceased. *Habitual lie. The fact that my mother lives seventy-five miles away and owns a country bar is totally irrelevant to my medical history. Plus, I've been listing her as deceased for the last five years...they'd think I was crazy if my mother suddenly came back to life.*
> Date of last period: *Oh God. This is why I'm here. It was right after Halloween, I remem-*

ber that. So that was November, and this is...?

January.

"Mrs. Devlin?"

I stand up and follow the nurse through the door into the maze of corridors. "Third door on the right," she says.

We go through the normal rigamarole, everything off, gown open in front. She takes a blood sample and leaves the room. A few minutes later Doctor Wilson comes in, flipping through my chart like it's the great American novel. With her long grey braid and her warm bed-side manner, she personifies Mother Nature. She's been my doctor forever. She held my hand the two times I miscarried, delivered Sofia, and did the LEEP procedure when they found precancerous cells on my uterus two years ago. She reminds me of the mother I wish I had.

"Thanks for squeezing me in today," I say.

She puts the paperwork down on her counter and stands close to me, her hand rubbing my arm. I am afraid I am going to cry.

"It's not everyday a woman turns forty," she says. "Happy Birthday."

I swallow. "Thanks. I haven't had my period in a couple of months and even though I took a home pregnancy test this morning and it was negative," I almost say *Eartha reminded me* but I catch myself just in time. "I remembered the same thing happened when I was pregnant with Sofia. So I thought I better come in."

"That's exactly what you should have done." There is a soft knock on the door and the nurse who drew my blood earlier hands Doctor Wilson a piece of paper.

Oh, God. I want to know.

I don't want to know.

Baby? Cancer? I'm not sure which scares me more.

Eartha starts singing quietly inside my chest. "Happy Birthday to me. Happy Birthday to me. Happy Birthday, dear Jodi, Happy Birthday to me."

"I've got news," Doctor Wilson says, reading the results from my blood test.

Nobody says "I've got news." They say, "I've got good news. Or I've got bad news." Not just news.

"You are pregnant," she says slowly.

"What?" I sit up fast. The paper under me makes loud throw-away noises and I feel nauseous.

"But your progesterone is low again."

I recite the words she told me all those years ago. They were burned into my brain. "It could mean I'm just low on progesterone and vaginal suppositories will take care of it. Or it's nature's way of ending an unviable pregnancy."

"Just until week twelve," she says gently. "You only have to take them until week twelve. If you get that far, things should be fine."

Fine? I can't imagine I'll ever be fine again.

She writes a number on a piece of paper. "I also think you should see a therapist. Someone to talk to. This isn't easy on any woman. I know you didn't want to see anyone last time, but I really think it's a good idea."

I'm forty. I'm pregnant. I'm high risk. I'm hearing voices.

I take the piece of paper.

Chapter Three

Jodi

I sit in the car, my hands on the steering wheel at ten and two even though I haven't put the key in the ignition, and stare out the windshield. I whisper the words out loud, "I am pregnant." The question hangs in the air like the cardboard pine tree dangling off my rear view mirror. Instead of making the air wintergreen fresh, though, the question sucks all the oxygen out of the closed car. I am pregnant...I am forty...I am pregnant and forty.

I can't decide which is more shocking, that I'm pregnant or the fact that I am not sure I want to be.

I feel like I am having an out of body experience. The me that is watching wants to jump in the backseat and tell my body to hit it...go, go, go! My spirit is off trying to find a time machine to transport me back to when I wanted this more than anything else. I rummage around in my psyche for my excitement, like a box packed away in the attic, with things you can't throw away even though you doubt you'll ever need them again.

It doesn't matter how many times I say it...it doesn't seem real.

Me...pregnant...now.

Maybe I misunderstood her. She must have said, "You're not pregnant."

No. She definitely said, "You *are* pregnant." And then she said my hormones are off.

That is what I get for not being excited. This is my punishment. I'm pregnant, but there's a chance that I won't be for long. I was pregnant twice before I had Sofia and lost them both times.

I hated that term, I lost the baby. Like I forgot and left it somewhere. I never lost a baby. I did everything I was supposed to and didn't get a baby.

Odds are, I won't get a baby this time either.

On the other hand, Murphy's law says that this time, simply because my first reaction is I am not sure I want it, this is the time I will go full term.

I was the child a mother didn't want and it completely shaped my life. I drop my head on the steering wheel, banging my forehead again and again. Deny, deny, deny that moment of clarity in the bathroom. It did not happen.

"Yes, it did." Eartha. Again.

"No it didn't!" I yell. No matter how loud I yell, I can still hear, or feel, that voice purring inside my chest.

"I don't want to be a mother again," Eartha says softly. "Not now."

"Stop saying that," I scream. "You have to love your baby. A mother should love her child more than herself!"

I hear her voice, or feel her voice, purring inside my chest. "I already did that," she says. "I loved, and still love, Sofia that way. But that doesn't mean I want to do it again."

"You can and you will." I put the key in the ignition and start the car. "You're just afraid. I don't blame you. I'm afraid, too."

"I don't have it in me to be the kind of mother you want to be," she confesses softly.

"Well, find it," I growl as I pull out of the parking lot.

Sofia is upstairs and I am making dinner. Of course I don't make what I want—wine and chocolate and more wine—so I make Sofia's favorite dinner...grilled cheese and tomato soup.

Truth be told, I don't make it because it's her favorite. I make it because it's easy.

Bob comes in from the garage, a huge bouquet of red roses in his hands. Probably forty roses. "Happy Birthday, honey," he says, giving me the flowers. "I thought about throwing you a surprise party tonight but Sofia convinced me you really meant it when you said you didn't want anything big." He kisses me and hands me a card. "I hope she was right."

I kiss him back, more for not throwing me a party than for the roses. I've already had more excitement than I can handle today. "Dinner last Saturday, at my favorite restaurant, with you and Sofia was the perfect celebration."

"Mom!" Sofia yells from the upstairs bathroom. "I need a towel."

I kiss him again, promising to open his card later, and climb the stairs like they're Mount Everest. I'm sure the reason she doesn't have a towel in the bathroom is that most of the towels are thrown on the floor in her room. I swear her hardwood floor is going to end up bowed from wet towels that were never hung up.

I grab a towel out of the linen closet. Knowing her modesty, at least where I am concerned, I open the bathroom door a few inches and hand in a towel as if I'm passing government secrets.

"Mom!" she cries indignantly. Apparently I should have squeezed the towel under the door.

I go back downstairs and study the bubbles in the tomato soup. We all prefer our soup made with milk, but I only had half a can of milk so I added half a can of water as well. It's not mixing well. Maybe I should have gone all water.

"Mom!" she yells again. "Did you do laundry today?"

"Sorry," I yell. "Didn't get to it."

I wilt under the weight of her sigh. I can't hear it, but I can feel her sigh through the floorboards.

Two minutes later. "Mom! Have you seen my white sneakers?"

"They're on the stairs."

She bounces down, then groans. "Not those," she says. "The ones with the pink laces."

How dumb am I?

Ten more seconds... "MOM!"

In the last fifteen minutes, she's called, "Mom," twelve times. Maybe I'll ask her to call me by my given name. I don't want to get rid of "Mom." I just want to remember what my name really is. It's my turn to yell upstairs to her. "Dinner's ready."

My fifteen year old daughter comes down the stairs wearing a tank top and a skirt that is so small I swear I have underwear that would cover more. I am surprised my eyeballs don't fall right out of my head and roll across the floor. I look at Bob, sitting at the table with his newspaper.

Normally, he leaves discipline to me; can't sully the father-daughter gag-fest of love they've got going on. Most of the time, I'm convinced the only reason they pretend to have this wonderful father-daughter bond is to bug me. Surely, this time, he'll be on my side. There's no way he'll let his princess leave the house looking like a tramp. A good-looking tramp, but a tramp none-the-less.

Then I catch her glance. I see that her eyes are challenging me, as if she can read my mind. As if she knows I remember when I didn't need a bra. When the right song could entice my breasts to break free and dance naked on ocean cliffs. When I still believed that secretly, inside, I really was part mermaid, part fairy, and part yet to be discovered.

Before the weight of life anchored me inside this middle-aged body that looks like every other middle aged woman. The one I swore I would never have. The body my daughter is looking at right now with complete disdain. And the utter conviction that she will never end up like me.

I wish I could flash forward in time and take a picture of her and bring it back to now and wave it in her face. Of course she will be me. She will be middle aged, with a husband hiding behind his paper, and a daughter staring at her with contempt,

If only I could tell her the truth, to enjoy what she has now, her youth, her vitality. That she doesn't need to flaunt it to the world. That it's hers, and it's temporary, and it should be savored. And cherished.

I'd also tell her that as much as she feels like she owns her power, it's not really hers; it's on loan. It's temporary and has a definite return date. And that date will be here long before she has the wisdom to appreciate it. It's only when it's gone, and she sees it standing in front of her in the form of her own daughter, that she will realize the magnitude of what she's lost.

I'd let her know that she doesn't need the world to tell her she's beautiful. That she doesn't need men to tell her she's amazing and bursting with life. That she should go back up to her room, take off all her clothes, and memorize the incredible beauty and fluidity of her body.

"I'm sorry," I say, for so much more than she can imagine, "but you cannot leave the house like that."

"Mom," she says, her voice an escalating whine. "This is what everyone wears,"

"Sofia Rose," I say, trying the full name thing.

She pulls the skirt down to cover some of her legs, thinking she's compromising but the effort loses it's effect when her belly gets exposed.

I look to Bob but he's still hiding behind his newspaper.

"C'mon, Mom," her tone vacillating as she decides on the direction of her argument.

"One," I say, a throwback to the days when she was young and I would count.

"Mom!" she yells, half of her daring me, challenging me.

I haven't used this strategy in years. "Two..."

"Seriously?" she yells.

We stare at each other, eyes wide. Neither of us is sure what the other is going to do. When she was young I never got past two so we never found out what happened at three.

Thankfully, she stomps back upstairs, muttering something about me ruining her life. That was close. I better not try this counting thing again because next time she won't respond out of habit.

Bob puts his paper down. "That's what you get for giving her a stripper's name."

Now? Now that she's gone he has something to say?

"I told you we should have named her Dylan. An androgynous name. If we had named her that, she'd be going to the debate club tonight dressed in baggy clothes."

"So it's my fault?" I demand.

"I'm not saying it's anyone's fault...."

"What are you saying?"

"I'm just saying...."

That's it. That's his answer to a lot of things. "I'm just saying...." And then nothing. There's never more to the sentence.

"WHAT?" I scream. "You're just saying WHAT?"

He folds his paper. "You're obviously not in a mood to talk, so I'll just leave you alone."

I'm so angry...so angry that I'm always the bad guy, that somehow I get stuck in the bad cop role even on my birthday. My anger is like a pinball game on speed, with all the little balls bouncing around and lighting up every one of my anger buttons but not stopping long enough to let off any steam...

That I let him go.

Chapter Four

Jodi

I put dinner on the table, mumble something about not being hungry, and go upstairs to our bedroom. I hear them put the television on and I don't even care. The fact that I have a bean bag chair tucked in the back of my walk-in closet is a testament that I sometimes hide in here from my family. I've got a book light, a small stack of romance novels, and a four pack of Kahlua™ White Russians.

I settle in, knowing I am hiding from a lot more than just my husband and my daughter today, although they are both on my avoid-at-all-cost list.

I'm also avoiding Eartha.

I unscrew a Kahlua drink. It's warm, but I'm not picky.

Then I remember I can't.

And why. I should be reading "What to Expect When You're Expecting." I devoured that book when I was pregnant with Sofia. Now I need a whole other book. "What to Expect When You Don't Know What to Expect."

Or..."What to Expect When Your Heart Takes on a Pop-Icon Personality and Starts Talking to You."

I can't drink. I can't read. So I pace.

When our builder gave us the option of having an en-suite bathroom or a walk-in closet, I begged, pleaded and did sexual favors for my new husband to get the walk-in closet. Of course the bedroom already had a standard closet. That was his.

This holy grail of closets was mine. All mine!

In my twenties, when I didn't have a lot of clothes, a huge walk-in closet seemed like heaven as I imagined my closet eventually filling with fabulous fashion.

Now, in my forties, with too many clothes, it's hell.

On the surface, my closet is organized. By season. By color. And ashamedly, by size.

My size sixes still don't take up much room. And then there are the eights. And the tens. It seemed the bigger the size, the more I needed of them, even though they were supposed to be temporary. And the twelves. And the new fourteens. And yet, I never have anything to wear.

At the time, I hated the eights. Now I look at them with such fondness and longing. The tens I called my terrible tens. Now I'd give anything to wear a ten. Even a twelve, at this point, would be a friend. My closet is a quicksand pit of self-loathing, but it's still good for hiding.

I walk around my closet-could-have-been-bathroom. Sure, I am hiding from my family. And my new friend. But mostly I'm trying to hide from myself, which is hard to do in a closet that haunts me with time passing. Of change. Of loss. Of all the things I am not anymore. I feel like my hourglass has broken and I'm trying to pick up the sand and put it back inside the broken glass. Time is leaking through my fingertips before I have time to live it the way I want. The way I had thought I would.

I miss time once it's passed more than I live it while it's here.

I push aside the shameful fourteens on the front rack and crawl to where the roof curves in toward the floor. Tucked back in the corner, right behind a box marked Halloween costumes, I find my pregnancy clothes. The first two times I was pregnant I took everyone's advice and held off on wearing maternity clothes. "You'll be so sick of them that you should wear your own clothes as long as you can." Since I miscarried at three months and at four months, I never got to wear them. That's why the third time when I was pregnant with Sofia, I started wearing the jeans with the elastic waist as soon as the plus sign was completely filled in. Every day that I managed to stay pregnant was a miracle and those maternity clothes were my armor.

Someone knocks on the closet door. For one second I wonder if Eartha would ever knock. "I'm naked," I say. That used to make Bob come running. Now my being naked is a non-issue. But it does keep Sofia away.

"No, you're not," Bob mumbles from the other side of the door.

I think about stripping everything off just to prove him wrong but I'd just have to put it all back on again.

"Gwen's here," he adds.

Why didn't he say that in the first place? I open the door and pull her into the closet with me.

My salvation. My pragmatic, no-nonsense, logical best friend. She will tell me why I am hearing Eartha, and what I should do, and—

Then I see her face.

She's been crying. And put too much make-up on to try to cover it. This isn't my best friend here, although she's trying. This is my best friend wearing a mask.

Takes one to know one.

This morning on the phone I was only thinking about my possible pregnancy in terms of me. I didn't think how it would effect her.

"What are you doing in here?" she asks.

"I'm hiding," I answer simply, offering her the bean bag. "From everyone, but you," I say with a smile.

"That's just because you can smell the banana nut muffins I made for your birthday," she says, handing me a Tupperware container. "I wanted to wish you a happy birthday. And check on you after our phone conversation this morning."

She's standing by the door, her hands shoved in her pockets. This closet would have been a terrible bathroom, way too awkward with two people in it at once. She can't ask me if I'm pregnant because my being pregnant will be one more reminder that she isn't. Here in my closet, amongst my fat and fatter clothes, I notice she is skinnier than ever, shrinking every year she doesn't grow with pregnancy.

I know she'll try to be here for me. Will want to be here for me.

But if I tell her that my heart is talking to me, and telling me I don't want to be pregnant, that will be too much for her to take. Because being pregnant is one thing, but being pregnant and not wanting to be, would be the ultimate betrayal.

"Nothing to worry about," I say. Not exactly a lie. The test I took at home this morning was negative. But what kind of friend lies to her best friend about being pregnant? Am I going to lose her when I can't hide the truth anymore?

She bends over and hugs me tight, then leans against the door again. Her posture is trying hard to be casual but her face is pulled tight. "I called a fertility clinic today. Since I've been tested and we know it's not me, it's obviously him."

"Gwen, maybe you just need more time."

"We've been trying for over two years. And he just refuses to get tested. So today after you and I talked on the phone, I got this crazy idea." She starts talking faster. "You know how he keeps saying he just wants to wait and see what happens? Well, what if I just went to the clinic," she says it casually, like she's suggesting going to the grocery store for milk, "and I could get inseminated. That way we could both get what we want. I could be pregnant and he could have his wait and see attitude." She holds her breath, her voice sounding funny. "What do you think?"

I repeat the question instead of answering it. "What do I think?" I peel the paper off a muffin and quickly fill my mouth. Another way of not responding.

"I'm not saying I'm doing it," she adds. "Of course I'll give it a few more months. It's just nice to know I have an option."

You mean a whopper of a secret, I want to say, but who am I to talk?

"If it came to that, of course it probably won't, but if it did, would you go with me?"

My mouth is still conveniently full so I just nod. "Thank you!" She opens the closet door, calling Happy Birthday over her shoulder. I sit down in my bean bag chair and peel the paper off another muffin. I realize I never even told her about Eartha as I take a delicious bite.

Maybe it's best not to mix real and imaginary friends anyway.

Chapter Five

Mel

I take a deep breath of fresh air before I press the doorbell to the nursing home, knowing it's the last full breath I will take for another hour until I come out again. If I breathe shallowly, I can pretend I don't notice the invasive smell of ammonia. I find it ironic that industrial strength cleaner and urine smell the same.

The door buzzes and I pull it open, waiting to make sure it closes and locks behind me. On this wing, the doors are locked because the patients wander off. Even with the locks, sometimes the patients, who most of the time are so out of it they can't feed themselves, manage to escape. Every once in a while, a sliver of lightening in time occurs and their brains get turned back on, almost with a super power strength. Three months ago Edie got out and walked almost three miles away in January, naked as the day she was born. Apparently, she snuck out hidden in the food cart.

When they asked her what she was doing, she said it was her husband's birthday, as if that explained everything. She leaned over to me and whispered, "Birthday sex," with a smile on her face. I know I'm not supposed to have favorites but I learned a long time ago that shoulds and should nots and I don't get along. If there's a should, then I don't want to. And if it's a should not, well not much is going to stop me. Some might say I have an opposite personality. I say the jack-ass who wrote the should book should be shot. Needless to say, Edie's one of my favorites.

By the time they got her back to her room, she had forgotten it was his birthday, forgotten where she was. More importantly, she had forgotten, once again, that her husband was dead.

I smile at the nurse sitting at the front desk as I walk by.

"They're all in the lounge waiting for you," she says, barely looking up. "Except Miss Edie. She's asleep."

"I'll stop by her room after I play," I say. The nurses call all the female patients by their first name with a Miss in front of it. Miss Edie. Miss Karen. Miss Dorothy. Reminds me of kindergarten. Respecting your elders, even when you have to change their diaper.

I walk into the lounge. Mr. Howard is twitching. He twitches twenty-four hours a day, even when he is asleep. Just watching him is exhausting. I rub his back for ten minutes and the twitching isn't quite so violent. His hand trembles as he reaches up and pats my hand. That's his signal that he's had enough. I think he's afraid if he stopped twitching completely he would die.

Patients in other wings of the nursing home have more visitors. Here, in the Altzheimer's wings, the patients are mostly abandoned. Old and demented apparently is a free pass to family members. Why visit someone who doesn't know who you are? Even as their brains are rotting inside them, their bodies fight to live. Sometimes I think it's because there's something they regret, something they have yet to finish. Other times I think it's just shit luck.

I step around Miss Stephanie. She grabs onto anyone or anything she can reach from her wheelchair and holds on so tight you end up dragging her along with you. It takes two nurses to get her gnarled hands off whatever, or whomever, she's got a hold of. I once saw her grab a little girl who was visiting one of the other patients. The little girl ran, screaming for her mother, dragging Miss Stephanie right along with her as if she could hitch a ride to somewhere else. "Good afternoon, Miss Stephanie," I say, keeping my distance, even though I don't blame her for trying to get out of here.

She grumbles, "I hate you but I love your shoes."

I take my seat on the piano bench and raise one foot. My red sequined ballet slipper glitters in the sunlight coming through the window. "If I let you wear them, will you dance while I play?"

"I hate the music. I hate the songs. I hate you."

Again, I don't blame her.

It's funny. When I come here, I feel vibrantly young. So alive I swear I can hear my own heartbeat dancing on the piano keys. Or, I feel sadness in the hollow of my bones. Literally aching that this terrible disease is ravaging these people who are all somebody's daughter, somebody's spouse, somebody's mother. So sad that I wish I could kill them and rob the devil of this living death.

So I do what I always do. I rub my hands and place them on the keys. "What are we all in the mood for?" I ask.

"A lullabye," Miss Dorothy says softly. "It's time for baby's nap."

She always says that.

Miss Dorothy leans forward, holding her doll out for me to see her. "Doesn't she have pretty red hair?" she asks me.

I nod in agreement. The doll is blonde.

"And those precious curls? She got those from her father."

The doll's hair is straight as a nail.

"You'd be pretty as a blonde," she says to me. "Red heads are trouble."

I brush my red hair out of my eyes. "I don't know about that, Miss Dorothy. I think a little bit of trouble is good for the soul." My fingers slowly start to play *Fly Me To The Moon.* I know it's her favorite song.

"That's the problem with trouble," she says, holding her baby close to her chest. "Where do you draw the line?"

My fingers dance softly across the keys and I wonder... Where do you draw the line, indeed?

The piano music has a soothing effect on everyone in the room, including myself. Music allows us to connect and be together without any of the pressure of trying to talk. After playing for half an hour, I go by Miss Edie's room for a visit. A while later I say my goodbyes and go out to my car. I have a habit I never break after volunteering at the nursing home on Mondays and Thursdays. I set the timer on my phone for ten minutes and sit with the windows wide open, regardless of the weather. And I do nothing but breathe.

I usually feel one of two ways...so depressed that I can barely move, wondering what the point of it all is if this is where we end up...

Or horny as hell. Live balls to the wall or why bother.

The ten minutes is usually enough time to get visions of taking a high dive off a bridge out of my mind. And enough time to stop me from calling Jake.

But not always.

The phone alarm dings. I take one more deep breathe and do an internal inventory...

Bridge…no.

Jake…probably shouldn't.

I dial anyway.

He picks up on the first ring. "I'm meeting the boys for rehearsal in an hour."

"That's ok," I answer. "I only need half that."

I hear the grin in his voice when he says, "C'mon over."

Just like I knew he would.

I lay on top of the sheets, my legs tangled with Jake's, one arm reaching across the bed and resting on his chest, my other forearm draped over my forehead. Sex was great. It always is with him.

But skin contact, now that is intoxicating. Jake knows me well enough, at least in bed, to not talk for a few minutes. No additional cuddling. Just the collapse of our bodies after the release, in whatever clumsy position we land in. I swear I can feel endorphins, little smiley faces floating on inner tubes through the lazy river of my bloodstream.

Breathing. So underrated. So simple. The only intimate relationship I really trust.

He rolls over and leans up on his elbow, breaking the silence. "How about after practice, we go out for a bite to eat?"

"I've got to work," I say.

"If I didn't know how handsome I am," he says, getting out of bed and picking his jeans up off the floor, "I might feel insecure that you never want to go out in public with me."

I laugh. "You being insecure is like calling The Queen Anne a row boat."

"I could be insulted that you use me for just a booty call."

I watch him pull on his jeans, always amazed at the beauty of his body. Even though he retired from the military long before I met him, he still has the body of a soldier. The strength. And the tenderness. "I'm your booty call too," I say, "and believe me, I am not insulted."

He sits on the edge of the bed to pull on his socks. I reach toward him to rub his back.

"What if I want more?" he asks quietly.

"When you want more," I answer simply, my hand dropping away, "you'll start looking for more."

He jumps on the bed and pretends to wrestle with me, rolling us over each other until he's on top. He grabs my wrists, holding them over my head. "Tell me one thing you like about me, besides my gorgeous body," he says, his blue eyes twinkling.

"Besides two hundred and twenty pounds of solid muscle?" I tease.

"There must be something else you like. It's been a couple of years."

"It hasn't been that long. And I only see you when you come into town."

"Thirty-six times," he says.

"You've been counting?" *Am I supposed to count?* I take a long breath in and exhale even slower. "I like that you are...." I pause, looking for the right word, "Sorry."

"You're sorry that you can't think of a single thing you like about me besides my body?" He lets go of my wrists, sitting up straight, still on top of me. "I'm appalled...and oddly flattered."

I throw a pillow at him. "I'm drawn to your regret."

He stares at me. I should have said his sense of humor, which I do like. Or his butt, which I really like. But those aren't my favorite thing about him.

"What makes you think I've done stuff I regret?" he asks softly.

"Haven't you?" Not quite knowing how the mood had taken such a somber turn, I add, "This is why we shouldn't talk. I'm not very good at it."

He lays down on me, his weight, his skin contact, melting us both into the mattress. "Mel, all joking aside. I am sorry. For a lot of things."

I wouldn't ask what for. I didn't need to know. And I don't want to be asked what I am sorry for. "I'm sorry, too," I whisper as I push off his jeans.

Between the sheets, with him, for tiny moments…I can feel the shadow of forgiveness.

Chapter Six

Jodi

I am in the bathroom staring at the one tiny square of toilet paper left on the what is that thing called?

"Honey, I got it!" Bob comes bursting into the bathroom. "I got the Japanese project."

"That's great," I mutter. I swear it's humanly impossible for any person in this house other than me to actually put a roll of toilet paper on the—

What is this damn thing called? Toilet paper holder? Toilet paper dispenser? Maybe if I could name it, I could make them change it.

"All these months of listening to those tapes," he says, practically dancing a jig in our small bathroom. "I'm gonna get a chance to use my Japanese."

I think I can speak Japanese. He swears by listening to it while he falls asleep he can learn it better. And God forbid I shut the tape off after he starts snoring so I could get some sleep. Our daughter can be throwing up in the bathroom and hubby will sleep like a baby, but shut his tape off even after he's snoring and he jumps up like a band of pillagers have stormed the bedroom. I wonder what the Japanese call this thing-a-ma-bob that holds the toilet paper? And I wonder if Japanese men and children are as allergic to replacing it as my family is.

"I'll be gone for two months," he says. "Maybe three."

"Gone where?"

"Japan. Haven't you been listening?"

I finally turn away from the toilet paper thingy and stare at my husband. "You're leaving me?"

He stops dancing. "I'm not leaving you."

"You just said you'd be gone for two months. Maybe three. Maybe forever."

"Jodi, I'm not leaving you. I'm going away for business."

TomAto, tomato. "You're leaving me." I close the toilet lid and sit down. Might as well use it as a chair since it's useless without toilet paper anyway.

"Do you want me to leave you?" he asks.

"What kind of question is that? I'm changing your goddamn toilet paper roll." I squeeze the thingy so I can take the empty cardboard roll off as if I'm showing a three year old how to tie his shoelace. "Would I be doing this if I wasn't your loving wife? Of course not. I'd let you get your own damn toilet paper."

"Does this mean you're going to miss me?" he asks, trying to tease a smile out of me.

I ignore his question obviously designed to make him feel better. "Of course I'll miss you," I'm supposed to coo. But I don't. Instead I ask, "What kind of man leaves his wife in my condition?"

"What condition?"

Take your pick...I'm old, and I'm pregnant, and I'm going crazy. I can't say the words out loud. I want to. I need to. But I can't. "What condition do I look like I'm in?"

He leans against the sink. "If you're talking about your mid-life crises that you've been going on about—"

I jump up. "And what if I am? You're going to leave me in a crisis?"

"I've tried to help you but you just keep telling me to leave you alone. I thought you'd love that I'm going to be gone for a bit."

"Is that what gets you to sleep at night? You're going because I want you to go?" I pretend to aim for the trash basket but the cardboard hits his knee instead. Truth be told, that isn't exactly where I was aiming either. "I want you to change the toilet paper! Just once, one lousy time in twenty years I'd like to be able to sit down and not have to check if there's any paper. I'd like for someone to think about what I need. To know that when I sit down to do my business, someone in this world loves me enough to make sure I have more than one tiny, little square of paper."

"I'll change the paper," he says, resigned.

"Sure you will." All I had to do was go a little crazy. This is our latest dance. I go crazy and he gets resigned. I don't want resigned, I want...

He looks around, as if the toilet paper is just going to magically appear.

"You don't even know where it is, do you?" I don't wait for him to admit his grievous sin. He doesn't have to. It's obvious he has no idea where to look. "If you were in a stranger's house and there wasn't any paper left, where would you look?"

"Under the sink?" He asks as if he has never run out of toilet paper in any bathroom ever. Does the world make sure he always has toilet paper wherever he goes? And conspires that there's never enough for me?

He bends down and opens the cabinet. "Nope."

"It should be there," I say slowly, "but someone used the last roll and didn't put it on the grocery list." I don't tell him that Sofia had propped the last roll on top of the back of the toilet. At least she knew where to look.

"In the linen closet?" he asks again.

"That would be a good place try next." I already know there isn't any in there either, but I'm not going to tell him. Let him deal with the idea that we only have one square left...who should get it? How will we survive?

He doesn't need to know I keep a family-sized package of eighteen rolls hidden in my closet for just this emergency. Let him sweat.

As he is walking out, he knocks over the trash can and suddenly he jumps back like there is a live grenade on the floor. I look down. Two tissues and a pregnancy test lay on the floor between us.

"What the hell is that?" he whispers horrified.

I guess now is the time to tell him.

His face drains of all color. If this is his reaction to a negative test, should I get him a brandy before I tell him the truth?

"Does she think by hiding it in our bathroom we won't notice it?"

Huh?

"Oh my God," he cries. "She's only fifteen."

He thinks it's Sofia's.

"Do you know about this?" he asks, pressing himself against the door when he can't back up anymore.

I shake my head. Why is he so sure it's hers? It doesn't even occur to him that it's mine? Never mind the fact that this morning I couldn't believe it either. Somehow, from him, it's insulting that he doesn't even consider it could be mine.

Sometimes the best way to stall is to go for the obvious. "It's negative," I say.

"So what? I mean, I guess that's good. But this means she's having sex. And probably not safe sex, if taking a pregnancy test is any measure. Maybe I shouldn't go to Japan."

"It's Gwen's." I don't know why I said that.

"What?"

And I don't know why I keep going. "That's why she came over last night. She didn't want to take it alone."

"Oh, thank God," he says.

"Thank God what? That it isn't our daughter's? Or that you can still go to Japan?"

"Thank God for both." He takes a deep breath. "If you don't want me to go, you know I won't go."

It's so easy for him to offer because he knows I'd never ask him to give up something he's worked so hard for. I try his favorite line. "I'm just saying..." I try to leave it there, try to say nothing else, but I can't. "You're leaving me."

He walks out of bathroom, shaking his head, and mumbling something about a close call.

He has no idea.

I close the door behind him and sit on the edge of the tub, my head in my hands. I am not even surprised when I hear Eartha ask, "Why didn't you tell him?"

Her voice is so near and so real I look up and honestly, I'm not surprised that she is sitting on my sink, crossing one leg over the other. I wonder if she can only appear in my bathroom, but I'm certainly not going to ask. "Why didn't you tell him?" I ask.

"Silly girl," she says, "he can't hear me. And even if he

could, you obviously didn't want to tell him."

"This isn't how I want to tell him. In a fight over toilet paper."

"Sounds like you better hurry up. Otherwise you'll be telling him he's going to be a Daddy over long distance."

"I'll tell him when, when," I stutter, not having any idea how to finish the sentence.

"When what? When you know how you feel?"

"I know how I feel," I say with false conviction. I have no idea how I feel.

"Of course you don't. I'm your heart and you won't even let me in on the secret."

"That's because," I say deliberately, "I'm not talking to you."

"What else is new," she says, studying her nails.

"What's that supposed to mean?"

"You haven't been talking to me for years. Why do you think I appeared on your fortieth birthday? I had to do something drastic to get your attention," Eartha purrs.

"Like I don't pay attention. I pay attention to everyone. I sympathize with everyone." I wave the spring loaded toilet paper holder in the air to make my point. "I understand Sofia is pulling away. Never mind the fact that every time she rejects me it feels like she is yanking a bandaid right off my heart. But it's what she's supposed to do, so I smile and pretend I'm happy she can't stand me anymore." I wrestle the spring thing back onto the wall, still empty. "And what about Gwen? I understand she can't handle that I'm pregnant, so I lied to her. Maybe I need someone to talk to!" I open the door stomp out of the bathroom, pretending I don't hear her say softly, "I'm here. I'm always here."

Seven

Jodi

I sit in the parking lot of the Boot-Scootin-Boogie and stare at the dimly lit bar. I know I shouldn't be here. I should go home and do something—anything—but sit here and be tempted.

I am ashamed that I am here. Embarrassed by my weakness, mortified by my need.

I get out of my car and open the trunk. Tucked way in the back is a plastic grocery bag that hides my disguise. I get back in my car and use the rear view mirror to put the wig on. Then I put on the reading glasses I don't need.

It's bad enough that I'm doing this. I can't do it looking like me.

I pull my leather jacket tight around me and walk toward the front door.

For a few minutes, half an hour at most, I will pretend I am not me. I will pretend I don't have this hole inside of me, the call that seems to be in my DNA no matter how hard I try to deny it. Most days, the call is so dim I can pretend it's not even there.

But when I'm weak, when I'm not sure, when I'm vulnerable, I can't deny the cry that is always in my blood...

I want my Mommy.

I take a seat in the corner of the bar, my head bowed low, and order a Cosmo from the waitress. Of course as soon as she leaves, I realize I can't drink it, but I don't want to call attention to myself by returning it.

I don't realize I am holding my breath until I see my mother coming through the swinging doors from the back. What little oxygen had been in my body freezes like little bubbles playing the Red-light Green-light game: the one where the person who is "it" faces a tree and yells Green-light, and you move forward until suddenly they turn around shouting, "Red-light!" If they see you moving, then you're it. And no one wants to be "it."

I sit at the bar, my hands wrapped tight around my glass of water, frozen in the Red-light zone. I am always conflicted when I see her. The logical part of me sees a friendly looking woman. The woman in me sees that long red hair. I wish I could get closer and look for roots. The jealous part of me wonders why I didn't inherit her hair. All this takes place on one side of my internal conflict.

On the other side is simply the echo…I want my Mom.

I hate that side. I hate that ache. Every time I come here I think this will be the time that I won't hear the call. This time I won't yearn to sit on her lap and bawl like a baby.

Does she even remember my birthday was yesterday? That forty years ago today she pushed me out into the cold world? Is she wishing she had let me have a real party with friends and balloons? That just once she got me a Little Mermaid Birthday cake instead of a Hostess Snowball Cupcake from the convenience store with a candle stuck in it, that she inevitably pulled out and used to light her cigarette?

I choke on my own tongue when I hear the first beats to the next song. I know it's one of her favorites. She runs out into the middle of the dance floor to lead the line dance. A cowboy croons over the speakers, "I like my women just a little on the trashy side."

You've got to be kidding me. The lullaby of my childhood.

How can she be out there dancing, having a good time, when I'm sitting here confused and scared? And why does my DNA pull me to her from seventy-five miles away and she doesn't even notice I'm in the room?

Eartha saunters up and sits on the stool beside me. There goes the hope that it's my house that is haunted, and not me.

"I expected a fire breathing dragon," she says, her foot tapping to the rhythm.

Believe it or not, I'm glad she's here. At least I don't feel so alone. And it's easy enough to talk to her in my head, since talking out loud to myself would definitely draw attention. "She probably lost that skill when she stopped downing pints of alcohol for breakfast."

"I thought she was a raging alcoholic?"

"She is. She's just not drinking now."

"Really? How come I don't know that?"

"Because all you need to know is she's still an alcoholic. Just because she stopped drinking doesn't mean she's cured."

"She doesn't look so bad." Eartha watches the dance floor. She probably wants to go out there and join the group. I swear I'll kill them both if she does.

I take a sip of water, wishing I could sip the Cosmo instead. "Not now, maybe. But you know she was a terrible mother."

"Your brain is rather selective on memories that it will share with me," she complains.

"Remember when we got our period?" I ask.

"At school, right?"

"Yes," I say slowly as if she's dim-witted. "Remember what happened at home?"

"It was a long time ago," she says, paying more attention to the dancers than me.

When the waitress brings my drink, I ask for a glass of water. In most ways, sixth grade seems like a life-time ago. But I remember that day.

Although I had understood the facts because of sex-education, I had been surprised, scared, and excited when I saw blood for the first time. It was near the end of the school day. I could hardly concentrate in class, knowing in my mind that every other girl was going through this at some point, maybe some other girl in my class was even getting it for the first time that day, but in my soul, in my body, I felt like I was the only one. I felt mysterious and powerful.

My Mom wasn't home after school, but the magical feeling continued. Even the slight cramping seemed a badge of honor that day.

By 6:00, Mom still wasn't home, so I fixed myself some canned spaghetti. To this day, canned spaghetti makes my stomach ache.

Mom still hadn't come home later that night when I went to bed. The next morning, there was a lot more blood and I couldn't go to school without something. I found my mother crumpled on the couch, using her coat for a blanket. Even though her make-up was smudged, she still looked like an angel, her long hair spread out like red-gold dust around her head. I knelt down beside her and gently shook her shoulder. "Mom?"

"Go away," she mutterred.

"Mom, I got my period."

Mom's eyes popped open and she stared at me intently. It was the moment I had been waiting for, the moment my Mom would really see me. The day we could share something.

Abruptly, Mom got up and I stayed kneeling by the couch, not sure what to do. Mom went into the bathroom. A minute later, she came out and threw a box of tissues at me. I barely had time to catch it. "Roll that up. If you're so grown up, you can buy your own tampons."

Eartha looks at me and I hate the pity I see in her eye. "That's a terrible way to transition into being a woman. I'm sorry," she says softly.

She isn't the one I want to hear it from. The woman I want to hear it from doesn't even know I am here.

I keep expecting to out-grow the urge to come here. That it's just a stage, like getting braces on your teeth. Eventually, they come off and you have a beautiful smile, completely forgetting that you ever had metal and elastics in your mouth. Yet here I am again.

I've had this fantasy that I would come here on my birthday. I would whip off my wig, throw back a shot of tequila and walk out without even paying for it. It would be my dramatic goodbye. And I would never come back.

Until this morning, that's exactly what I intended to do. The fact that I intended to do it on my twentieth birthday, and my thirtieth, and my thirty-fifth has no bearing on the fact that I really was going to do it today...

Until I found out I was pregnant.

And I don't know how I feel about it.

And I'm terrified because it could mean...

I am more like her than I can bear.

Chapter Eight

Jodi

I have to get a handle on how I feel about being pregnant. Since I'm too confused to talk to the people I love, I make a preemptive strike for sanity. I call the therapist on the card Doctor Wilson gave me, which is why I'm now sitting in the reception area waiting for my turn to cry on the proverbial couch.

Her white noise machine makes me think about getting one for my bathroom in case Eartha decides to show up again. Totally passive aggressive, but I'm fine with that.

Doctor Madelyn LaPointe opens her door and invites me into her office. I follow her in. Already I don't like her office—way too cheery. And I don't like her rate—way too expensive. Finally, I don't like her hair. How am I supposed to trust a woman whose hair reminds me of Medusa with wild curls going every which way?

I sit in one of the armchairs with the cheerful daisy slip-covers. I expect her to sit in the big leather chair behind the desk but instead she sits opposite me in the matching chair. I imagine she does this to make me feel more comfortable, like we're old friends getting together to chat. But friends don't have my paperwork resting on their lap, politely covered with a blank yellow-lined legal pad. Or a pencil ready to take notes on my crazy. But I'm here now so I start to talk. "Doctor LaPointe—"

"You can call me Madelyn." She smiles and nods. I swear one of her curls slithers around her neck and I wonder if she is going to be choked by her own hair before I can get fixed. I talk faster. "I went to the doctor because I haven't had my period. I thought it was early menopause. Surprise. I'm pregnant."

"Wow," she says, her curls applauding.

That's it? Wow? Where's the congratulations? Where are all the normal questions you ask a woman when she tells you you're pregnant?

Instead, she asks, "How do you feel about that?"

Seriously? How do I feel? She's going to have to do better than that for one hundred and twenty-five dollars an hour. "Well, my hormones are low. Doctor Wilson said it could be I'm just low on progesterone and the supplements will take care of it. Or it might be nature's way of ending an unviable pregnancy. I just have to wait and see."

"That's a difficult place to be."

"I know. I've been here before." I take a deep breath. "I know what it's like to be pregnant and know it doesn't look good, and you want it more than anything. That's not what I'm feeling." Saying what I *don't* feel is as close as I can come to actually saying what I do feel.

"So what are you feeling?" she asks.

Apparently she's on to my game. "I know what I should be feeling. I should be ecstatic. Thrilled beyond belief that I'm getting what I've wanted for so long. And petrified that it might get taken away."

"And you're concerned because that you're not feeling all that?" she asks.

"Of course. I must be crazy if I'm not."

"You've been through this before," she said gently, flipping through the paperwork I had filled out when I first came in. "I see you have had two miscarriages. So you are being cautious with your feelings this time. There's nothing wrong with that."

I fidget with my rings in the quiet moment. "I just can't believe I'm pregnant. And..." I whisper the next word, ashamed. "Ambivalent."

"Sounds healthy...a wait and see attitude. Are you doing everything the doctor wants you to?"

"Of course."

She smiles. "Then this is one more thing you're doing right for both of you."

"How can you say ambivalence about being pregnant is good? Do I use the red or the green tablecloth at Christmas? That's a thing to be ambivalent about. Do I fantasize about Hugh Jackman from Wolverine or one of his other movies tonight? Do I want to be pregnant, when I am, is not the thing to be ambivalent about!"

"You have medical reasons to know this pregnancy isn't in the clear yet. Why not wait until you know how it's going?"

"Because that's too late..."

"Too late for what?" she asks. "Are you thinking about terminating?"

"How dare you ask me that?" I start crying. "Do I sound like a woman who would...would even think about..."

"What are your feelings about abortion?"

"In my head, I think it's a woman's choice. But in my heart, I would never."

"Oh yes, I would," Eartha pipes up. I turn my head slightly and see her sitting in the chair in the corner.

Eartha, shut up! "No you wouldn't." I realize I'm talking to Eartha out loud. "I mean, I wouldn't. And abortion isn't the worst thing I could do anyway."

"What is?" she asks gently. "What is the worst thing you could do?"

"Have a child I don't want," I whisper.

"The fact that you are confused about your feelings, one day after you found out your are pregnant and high risk, doesn't necessarily mean you don't want the baby. You need time to process. Both the information and your emotions."

"These emotions can't be mine," I argue. "It's like they're coming at me from out of the blue. Like someone else's sock ended up in my dryer. I have no idea where they came from."

She pauses for a moment. "I bet you have some idea where they are coming from."

No way I'm going to touch that one. "Here I am, comparing my emotions to stranger's sock showing up in the dryer of my life. That's nuts."

She writes something on her pad of paper. "So let me make sure I have this. You think you're crazy."

"Exactly. I've got enough reasons to be."

"Do you want me to say you're crazy?"

"That would be better than not caring."

She tucks a wayward curl behind her ear. "After seeing you for only a few minutes, already I would say you're not crazy. And you're not numb, although I think you wish you were. And I don't even think you are ambivalent about being pregnant, although again I think maybe you wish you were. I think you're afraid to know what you really are." She leans back in her chair and crosses her legs. "I think my job is to help you figure out how you feel."

"I don't want to know how I feel."

Eartha pipes in again. "Yes, we do."

I ignore her. "I want to know if I'm crazy."

Doctor LaPointe smiles again. "I can tell you right now you're not crazy."

I am disappointed. Crazy I can deal with.

"So we can sit here and stare at each other for the next forty-five minutes, or we can talk about how you feel."

"I told you, I don't feel anything yet."

"In the last twenty-four hours you turned forty and you found out you're pregnant. I can almost guarantee that you're feeling a whole jumble of emotions. And it's completely understandable if you're confused about how you feel."

I pull a pillow from behind my back that is making me uncomfortable and hug it to my chest. "I wish I felt a lot of things."

"Jodi, you're pregnant and you're high-risk pregnant. You turned forty yesterday. Maybe the real question is...why don't you want to know what you feel?"

"This morning I almost threw my coffee pot away."

"Okay," she says, making a quick note on her pad of paper. "Let's start there. Why?"

"Every other time I got pregnant, I put my coffee maker away under the counter for nine months. This morning I thought I should throw it away because I knew I'd be tempted. I'd done everything right before, and it didn't make any difference. I knew that one morning I would wake up and I would want coffee. I'm not sure I can trust myself not to have one."

"You know having a cup of coffee won't cause a miscarriage," she says gently.

"That's the whole point. It feels like nothing I do matters. Like I have no control."

"Knowing everything isn't in your control can make you feel better," she offers.

"Or it can make you feel worse," I say, resigned.

"You keep saying wanted and tried, all past tense. When did you stop trying?"

"I never stopped. It's more like I gave up. A couple of years ago, when my period was a minute late, I took what was probably my five hundredth home test and as I was sitting there counting the seconds until I could look, I got mad. I got so angry I was shaking. I broke that test right in half before it could scream, 'Not Pregnant' at me. I stopped wanting a baby because I couldn't have one."

Doctor LaPointe tipped her head to the side. "If I had a magic ball and said everything was going to work out, how would you feel then?"

I can feel words crawling around my stomach...

Scared.

Happy.

Nauseous.

None of them will come out though because they're not really right. They'd make sense. They'd be understandable, but they don't fit. Those words feel like tiny gallstones stuck in my gut.

"Tricked," I whisper, clapping my hand over my mouth. I heard the word before I knew I was going to say it.

"Tricked?" she asks.

"I wanted this for so long and couldn't have it. I don't know if I want it anymore." Oh my God. "A mother is supposed to love her child more than anything, and I just don't know if I have that kind of love in me anymore."

"Who says what a mother is supposed to do?" she asks.

"I say." I swallow. "And I swear if I do have this baby, I will love it. But I'm afraid I won't love it right."

"What do you mean by right?"

"I would take care of it. I would get up in the middle of the night. I would save for it's college education." I am quiet for a moment. "When Sofia was born, I would do anything for her. It was the purest love I've ever felt."

She lifts the legal and looks at my chart. "Your daughter is fifteen, right? Do you love her like that now?"

"Of course I do..."

"I hear a but..."

"I love her, but I don't always like her. And I used to love the kind of Mom I was. Now I'm a pathetic cliché of a frustrated mother with a teenager."

"So love is messy," she says. "It's easy to love when things go as we plan. Some would say real growth happens in the messy parts."

"I don't like messy love. Isn't that pure love I felt when Sofia was born what life is supposed to be about?"

"That is part of life, yes. But the messy love, the love you still have for Sofia, the confusion you have about this pregnancy, this is what life is about, too."

I shift in my chair, wondering why the more comfortable a chair looks, the more uncomfortable it usually feels. "If I'm just going to end up here in fifteen years, almost looking forward to my kid going off to college, what's the point?"

She looks down at her notes then back at me. "So you were angry you couldn't have another baby."

"Of course I was. There are lots of women who become mothers who shouldn't. Women and girls who get pregnant by mistake. More than once. And there I was, ready and willing to be a great Mom, and I couldn't. That doesn't seem fair."

"It isn't fair," she says.

I'm surprised how good it feels to have someone else say it out loud. "I didn't stop wanting another baby. But I had accepted I couldn't have another one."

"Maybe you found peace in that acceptance."

"Peace?" For a second there, I thought she understood me. "That sounds like I was happy with it. No. I accepted it. Unwillingly."

"I'm sure you were angry for a long time," she says. I can tell she's offering me a bone, trying to tease me like a dog out into the yard, but as soon as I go, she's going to slam the door shut and leave me out here alone.

"You identified yourself as woman who was denied another child," she continued. "Maybe you don't want to give up that anger."

"First you think I'm in peace. Now you think I'm stuck in anger." I stare at her. "Why would I resist knowing peace?"

"It would mean letting go of an identity. And Ego thrives on identity. There was power, and drama, and angst in being a woman who couldn't have another baby. You saw yourself as a victim of your own womanhood that denied you a second child. So even though there's peace in accepting, there's also letting go. You probably wanted the peace, but not the letting go."

We are both quiet. I know she's giving me a chance to digest what she said. Peace is tempting, but it also means admitting—

"It's okay to acknowledge you're finding it, let's say unsettling, to be pregnant."

I can handle the word unsettling. It's so neutral. Unemotional. "If we didn't want a baby, we should have been using protection."

She shrugs one shoulder. "Sounds like with your past, you didn't really believe it could happen."

"Well, it's happened. I'm pregnant. And you just know Murphy is having a good old time up there."

"Murphy?"

I shove the pillow back on the chair behind me. "You know, Murphy's Law. This time, things will move along smoothly."

"So...you aren't sure you want this." She says it as a statement, but I can hear the question in her words, can see her pencil just waiting to write down my answer. To put it into writing. To make it real.

"I never said that." I watch the large hand on the clock move to twelve and I can almost hear the click saying my time is up.

Chapter Nine

Jodi

I come into the house and drop my purse on the counter, exhausted beyond belief. I reach into the fridge and when I close the door, I practically have a heart attack—Jack Nicholson is standing on my dining room table like it's a courtroom pulpit. "You can't handle the truth," he screams just like he did in *A Few Good Men*.

What the hell?

"I'm not telling you the truth because," he says, pausing for dramatic effect, "You can't handle the truth!"

"Fine," I mutter, pulling the peanut butter out of the cabinet. I stab my knife inside the jar and try to spread it, ripping the bread in the process. Now the jelly is going to leak out all over me. I grab a banana off the counter and slice it up. "I can't handle the truth," I mumble. The fact of the matter is I can't handle another vision, or haunting, or whatever this is. Why can't I get Gandhi? Or Maya Angelou? Even Oprah. Why am I being stalked by pop icons?

I grab a small bag of Fritos and walk into the living room, picking up the remote and turning the television on, hoping Jack will take the hint and leave me alone.

No such luck.

"What kind of limp-dick answer is that?" he asks, following me into the living room. "You should demand the truth."

I mute the television. "What if I don't want the truth?"

"Why didn't you tell Gwen that you don't agree with what she's doing?"

"She didn't ask for my opinion." I take a bite of my sandwich. It's good. And healthier with a banana instead of jelly. I haven't had one of these since I was pregnant with Sofia.

"If Gwen did ask for your opinion, would you give it?"

"I am not going to tell her I think going to a clinic behind her husband's back is wrong. She doesn't want to hear that."

"It might not be what she wants to hear but it's exactly what she needs to hear. Isn't that what a real friend would do when she sees her friend heading down the wrong road?"

I push my sandwich aside and open the bag of Fritos. "She wants a baby." Yum...salt. I lick more off my fingers.

"Do you think what she's doing is right? Lying to her husband, lying to her baby about who father really is?"

"First of all," I say, "she didn't say she was doing it. Just that it's an option."

He takes the remote and starts switching channels. "She didn't say she was joking, either," he says.

"I admit, she's a bit obsessed. But that's because she wants it so much. I don't think she's seeing the forest for the trees."

"She's lying to her husband, lying to her future baby out who the father really is. Involving you in her dirty little secret and asking you to lie to both of them for the rest of their lives."

"Do you know something I don't?" I look at him suspiciously. "Is she going to do it?" I ask. "Is she going to get pregnant?"

"How should I know?" He grabs the Fritos and starts shoving them into his mouth. Since when can visions eat?

Note to self, next vision, or whatever this is, should be a fortune teller. At least then I could learn something about the future. Or buy a lottery ticket.

"I'm not against getting help," he says. "I'm against lying to a man about a baby. Telling him it's his when it really isn't. Tricking him into fatherhood."

"Of course you think that. You're a man. You'd always side with the man. He wants a baby, too. But he refuses to get checked. So I don't see how this is hurting him." It's fun playing devil's advocate with Jack.

"Maybe this way would be okay with him. But he has a right to know."

"I tried to talk to her—"

"Bullshit!"

"I did." Why am I defending myself? Part of me agrees with what he's saying but I'm sure as hell not going to tell him that.

"You lie to her about you. You lie to her about her. Interesting take on friendship."

I take the bag of Fritos back from him before he eats them all. "What do you know of friendship? In that movie with Helen Hunt—"

"*As Good As It Gets*," he interrupts me.

"—you were a terrible neighbor and friend." I never really understood his appeal. Seems to me he always played a freaking lunatic.

"We're not talking about me and my career. We're talking about you. When she asked if you would go with her, why didn't you refuse to go?"

"Because she asked me to go."

"If she asked you to jump off a cliff, would you?"

"How about if I ask you? Will you jump off a cliff?"

He shrugs his shoulders and leans back on the couch, folding his hands across his bulging belly.

Why couldn't George Clooney show up in my living room? Or Antonio Banderas? Or—

"So...when are you going to tell hubby about the baby?"

I was hoping he didn't know. I should have known better. "Tonight," I answer.

"Really?"

I nod. I hadn't planned on it, but I do need to. And I can tell it's the last thing Jack expected me to say. There is some satisfaction in surprising him.

"Yes. I'm going to set the mood. Maybe make love. And then I'll tell him." Make love? Yuck...since when do I call it that? Bob and I have sex. Or we fool around. Only people in movies make love.

"What do you think he's going to say?" he asks, a question I haven't let myself think about.

"He'll be thrilled, of course." I go back into the kitchen for more Fritos. "If it's a boy," I say over my shoulder, "we're going to name him Batman."

Jack laughs. "Very funny. Maybe when you finish with this mother gig, you can become a comedy writer."

At this point, I think the mother thing is either going to last forever, or it's going to kill me.

It's a toss-up which will come first.

I'm laying on my side of the bed, wide awake beside my sleeping husband when Jack breaks his head through my closet door like in *The Shining*. "Here's Johnny!" he says, smashing through the splinters of what's left of my door. I notice he's made up like the Joker. Guess he's getting his movies confused.

Bob's already snoring so I know he won't hear Johnny breaking my closet door. Or me talking to my imaginary friend. Unless, of course, I shut off his incessant Japanese CD.

Jack's a good distraction. I'm so in the mood to break something, I wish I could crash through doors.

Johnny, aka the Joker, saunters into the bedroom, folds his hands in front of his chest and bows. "Kon'nichiwa," he says in perfect Japanese. "So what does Bob think of being a daddy again?"

I pull my old robe around me over my nightie. "I don't know."

"I thought you were going to tell him tonight."

"I was. I tried. You think I'm wearing this stupid teddy-nightgown for my own pleasure? The fact that I still have it on should tell you the night didn't go the way I planned." I sit on the edge of the bed. "I tried to tell him."

He raises one overly made-up eyebrow. "You try to tell people a lot of stuff. And you blame them for not hearing. But you rarely say what you really mean."

"I lit candles. Had Barry White on the CD player. Even put this stupid lacy nightgown on. Thought we could have sex, you know the thing that got us here in the first place. Then afterwards, in the after-glow, I'd tell him."

He sits on the edge of the bed beside me. "Good Plan A."

"He turned me down. Said he was distracted. That sleeping with me is what he's going to miss while he's away." I pretend to gag. "He's leaving for God-knows-how-long and he just wants to snuggle?"

Jack pulls a small notepad out of the inside pocket of his jacket pocket. He stands up and pulls a lead pencil out of his other pocket. He dabs the tip of the pencil on his tongue with a big flourish.

"What are you doing?" I ask.

"Those are some good lines. It's sleeping with you I'm going to miss more than anything. A lot of women would probably find that romantic. Get me some tail."

I continue repeating what Bob had said. "I've slept with you every night for the past eighteen years," I say, mimicking my husband, "I wonder if I'll be able to sleep without you."

Jack stops writing. "Getting a little corny for my taste." He stares at me, one eyebrow-raised. "If you wanted his attention, maybe you should have bought a Japanese porno. Then he could be learning and having sex at the same time. The ultimate multitasking." Jack flips to a fresh page and slices a line down the middle of the new page. He says our names out loud as he writes them at the top of the columns. He studies it for a second, then looks up at me. "On the scorecard of marriage, you're way ahead."

Finally, he's on my side. "I never thought of it that way, but you're exactly right." Jack frowns. At least I think he does. It's hard to tell with that huge smile painted on his face.

"Let me say it again. On the scorecard—"

"What? You think I should tell Bob that Jack Nicholson thinks I'm trying harder at our marriage than he is?"

"Do you think it's healthy to have a scorecard? Friendship is about lies, and marriage about points? And according to you, you're so far ahead it's like Babe Ruth playing against the Little League."

"At least I'm trying," I defend myself. He laughs so loud I am tempted to tell him to keep it down.

"You pretended you wanted sex," he says, "then got all self-righteous when you didn't get it."

"Yeah, well, that's more than he did. What did he do?"

"He shared what he wanted with you. He was honest."

I roll my eyes. "Now wanting to cuddle gets an A for effort?"

"What did you want?" he asks.

I don't say anything.

"Did you want sex?"

"Not really," I admit.

"But you went for it anyway." He deducts a point from my column. "Did you want to cuddle with him tonight?"

"Not right then, no. I was too pissed."

"But ya did." Another point lost.

Pencil poised, he asks, "Did you tell him now might not be the best time to go to Japan?"

I shrug a shoulder. "Sort of. But I can't wait for him to go, too."

"Why not tell him both?"

"Yeah, that's what I should say. 'Honey, I don't want you to go, but could you hurry up and go?' That's not very nice."

He flips the notebook closed and puts it back in his jacket pocket. "Is that why your default setting is to always do what you think you're supposed to do?"

"Fuck off!" I say.

He grins. "Feels good to say how you feel, doesn't it?"

"You're an idiot."

He grins some more. "No, I'm a Pisces."

I'm guessing that's a line from one of his movies.

"You ever dance with the devil in the pale moonlight?" he asks, clearly in character.

"What?"

He claps his hands. "Oh, goody, you know your line."

I shake my head.

"I say, 'You ever dance with the devil in the pale moonlight?' and you say, 'What?' and then I say, 'I always ask that of my prey.'"

"Oh, I get it. The Batman movie." I pull the belt of my robe tighter. "But I'm not your prey."

"No. But I am your truth. And I am here whether you like me or not."

"Well, I don't like you," I say. "Or your truth."

"I'm *your* truth." He smiles. Or keeps smiling. It's hard to tell with that smile drawn on his face in clown make-up. "Don't worry. I'll grow on you." He sits down beside me and believe it or not, I kinda like his company. For some reason, I don't feel like I have to pretend with him. Or be nice. It's very liberating.

"You don't trust anyone to care about you enough to take care of your needs," he says. "And I think me and Eartha are showing up cuz you don't even trust yourself."

I smile. "I'd never swear at Eartha...She's too much of a lady."

"You show up. But you don't really share yourself."

"I share." I mumble. I'm tired. Pregnant women get tired."

"You've been tired for years. What are you...pregnant with an elephant?"

I laugh.

"This town needs an enema!" he declares with a flourish.

Obviously another line from a script.

"And by town," he adds, "I mean you." He kisses me on the cheek and walks out of the room whistling.

I lay back down beside Bob. Even in his sleep, his knee lifts up a little so I can wiggle my way under his weight and burrow into his heat. Who knew that arguing with Jack was just the release I needed tonight. Just before I drift off, I turn around. My closet door is, of course, completely intact.

Chapter Ten

Jodi

I'm back on my therapist's couch, which in her case is a big comfy chair covered in fabric with big flowers. Obviously, I am desperate. I have to ask someone why the hell Eartha Kitt is showing up at my house. And Jack Nicholson. But I'm not sure where to start.

"Last time you were here," Doctor LaPointe says, "you weren't sure how you were feeling. Do you know more today?"

For crying out loud, it was only a few days ago. "Not really."

"Okay, then. How does your husband feel about having a baby at this point in life?"

"I haven't told him yet."

"Why not?"

"Because he's going to be fine with it. He'll just go with the flow. And that will piss me off so much I'm afraid I will kill him."

She just sits there.

"Not kill him for real," I explain. *Kill him like I killed my mother.*

She smiles. "I wasn't about to call the police."

"But if I did kill him, and I got a jury of my peers, other middle-aged women with easy-going husbands, I'd be acquitted."

"Why does his easy going attitude bother you?" she asks, the yellow legal pad poised on her lap.

"Because if he's fine if we do, and fine if we don't, then he must not care. If he really wanted something and couldn't have it, wouldn't it make sense that he'd be upset?"

"But we don't always get everything we want," she says.

"I know. So you try harder."

"Sometimes it isn't about trying."

"I hate that! If you try hard enough, if you just try hard enough, life should....."

"Was there something you wanted in life? Something you tried, and no matter how hard you tried, it was never enough?"

"We're not here to talk about what I didn't get, we're here to talk about what I did get. Pregnant." And imaginary friends. Just haven't quite figured out how to bring that up.

"Okay. What about Sofia? How do you think she will feel?"

"When she was little, she wanted a baby sister. The summer she was eight years old she played baseball at camp and decided she wanted a brother." I shrug my shoulders. "So she used to want one."

"Sound familiar?" Doctor LaPointe asks. "What do you think she'll say now?"

"Now it will probably be an affront to her. She'll be even more embarrassed by me."

Doctor LaPointe takes a slow, deep breath and I find myself mimicking her. I wonder if she does that on purpose.

"Maybe telling your family will comfort you," she says. "You'll realize you're not in this alone."

I wilt into her daisy chair. On the floor near her door between her office and the reception area, her sound machine emits a wind noise that drones on and on. I know it's there to protect my privacy. Like anyone who isn't being paid would want to listen to this. "I can't tell anyone I am pregnant until I can be sure I'm happy about it. And you can't ask me to be happy about it while my hormones are off. Once I know, one way or the other...."

"Finding out the healthiness of this pregnancy might not make all your feelings clear." She leans forward. "Why isn't it okay that you're confused? That your emotions are all over the place. It seems to me this is a normal reaction. There isn't a right or wrong way to feel," she says gently, trying to convince me.

"I know the world isn't black and white, but there are a few black and whites you should be able to count on."

She leans forward and I'm surprised her notebook doesn't fall off her lap. "Give me one," she says.

"A mother is supposed to love her child more than anything."

"But that isn't always the truth, is it?"

I know that better than anyone. "But I want to count on it. It's one of my black and whites."

"And you're finding yourself lost in the grey." She flips through the papers I filled out yesterday looking for the rest of my family. "I see your mother is dead."

Is nothing else interesting on my form? I have a life beyond my mother is dead...*when she isn't.*

But she doesn't know that. "Yes. She died five years ago. We were really close."

"I'm sorry. That must have been tough."

I nod. "We used to talk on the phone every day. On Thursday nights, we took a pottery class together. I still have the lamp she started but didn't get to finish."

"You're lucky you had such a close relationship with your mother," she says.

I am not sure I like her tone. Almost like she doesn't believe me. I call on one of the few good, real memories I have with my mother. "When I was little and I was sick, she'd make hot chocolate for me. And she'd put a butterscotch stick in it that I used to stir in the whipped cream."

Doctor LaPointe, I refuse to call her Madelyn, makes a note on my chart. "Sometimes part of why we become a mother is to right the wrongs of our own mother."

"Aren't you listening? My mother was perfect."

She is quiet for a moment. "Then maybe one of the reasons you thought you wanted to have a baby is because you miss your mother?"

"Yesterday you were telling me I didn't want a baby."

"I didn't say that. You did. I think there is a part of you that is still holding onto the idea of another chance. I'm just wondering," she asks, looking at me closely, "another chance at what?"

"I certainly did not get pregnant to replace my mother," I say with a little too much gusto.

"There must have been something your mother—"

"If you're one of those therapists who think everything is your mother's fault—"

"Of course I don't think that. But I do think they have a big impact on our lives."

"I don't want to speak ill of the dead." *Or the un-dead.* I take a deep breath. "Can you put the pencil down, please? You can't write this next thing."

"Why not?"

"Because it will make me look crazy."

She smiles. "Okay." She puts the pencil down on top

of her clipboard.

"My mother's not dead."

She waits. I swear her fingers twitch, wanting that pencil, but I am impressed that she resists. "And we didn't have a perfect relationship. Pretty much the opposite of everything I said."

Her hair twitches as she picks up her pencil again. "Not having a perfect relationship with your mother doesn't make you crazy."

I sigh and pull at a loose thread on my jeans. "We don't have a relationship at all."

"So the question stands...do you want another baby because you miss your mother?"

"Why would I miss what I don't even like?" I ask. I can't help but notice the first page on her pad is almost full.

She stops writing. "Maybe you don't miss what you had, but you miss what you wanted."

"I am not here to talk about my mother."

She smiles. "Then maybe you shouldn't put she's dead on your forms."

"Don't you think that's a hint that I don't want to talk about her?"

"I think it's the exact opposite," she says, barely looking up she is writing so fast.

I look at the clock. Time to go.

I hate therapy.

I stand over the grill on the back porch and pour more lighter fluid on the coals. I need a good hot fire to get this mother thing under control.

I don't need therapy. And I don't need my mother. I

add a few twigs I picked up from the yard to the fire. I am going to have a symbolic cleansing ceremony. I am going to burn the wig I've used as my disguise. No more hiding. No more pretending I'm ever going to go to her bar and have some dramatic moment with her. Time to move on.

I squeeze more lighter fluid and watch the orange and blue flames dance higher, feeling like a snake charmer enticing the cobra out of the basket. "This ceremony represents my letting go of my anger toward my mother," I say to the flame, feeling very new age-y. "I will burn away all desire for my mother," I announce to the back yard. I turn around and look for the wig that I draped over the chair behind me.

Where the hell is my wig?

I turn back to the fire and Eartha is sitting on the railing around our deck caressing the wig like she's petting a cat. She sitting side-saddle in her tight sequin dress. Doesn't the woman own a pair of jeans?

"Give me that," I say, pulling the wig out of her hands.

"Did you pick one that looked like her hair on purpose?" she asks.

I look at the wig. "What are you talking about?"

"That wig...it looks just like your mother's hair."

"This is nothing like my mother's hair." The hair I have always secretly envied.

"Just because it's long, and strawberry blonde...." I trail off.

"Actually, it's way more red than blonde. Just like your mother's." She leans back and studies me for a moment. "Now that I think about it, you looked a lot like her when you were wearing it."

Talk about adding insult to injury. I picked a disguise to hide from my mother that made me look like her? "My mother had beautiful hair. She still has beautiful hair. You'd think all those years of hard drinking would have robbed her of her looks, but she's still quite pretty." It's amazing how much easier it is to tell the truth to someone who isn't real. "There's something about her. That 'it' factor. She has that. She always has."

"And you don't think you have 'it'"?"

"That's the thing about motherhood," I say. "It's a supporting role. If you do your job right, no one notices you."

Eartha leans back, her face toward the sun. "But womanhood is different than motherhood. That's why I only had one baby. I knew if I had anymore, I would lose myself and I love me too much to lose me."

I try not to ask her to elaborate, but I can't help myself. "So how is womanhood different than motherhood?"

"You basically said being a mother makes you invisible," she says, her voice always a sensual, rolling song. "If you do being a woman right," she purrs, "no one forgets you." All of a sudden, Eartha is dressed in tight black leggings and high boots.

"What are you?" I ask. "A fashion shifter instead of a shape shifter?"

She whistles and a white stallion comes running out of the woods. "I have the urge to ride," she says, jumping on it's back, no saddle, straddling the horse and riding around the back yard, her laugh echoing through the trees.

"Why can't we do both?" I whisper, the question coming out on a breath and dissipating into thin air. "Be a good mother and be unforgettable." I shake my head. This is supposed to be my cleansing ceremony, not Eartha's day at the circus. "You should be proud of me," I yell to Eartha as she circles past. "I've realized I am holding on to the past a little too tightly."

She pulls the reins in and leaps back onto the porch,

walking the railing like a tight rope as her horse gallops back into the woods. "Honey, my bra is a little too tight. Your grip on the past is more like boa. And I don't mean the feathery kind." Suddenly she has a black feather boa in her hands that she dramatically throws over one shoulder. "Maybe you could do more than let go. Maybe you could forgive her."

I finger comb the hair, making it neat again. "Forgive her? Why the hell would I do that?"

"Don't do it for her. Do it for you."

It's hard to take philosophical advice from a circus performer balancing on my deck rail. "Do I look like forgiving her would be good for me?"

"If you don't forgive her, you can't forgive yourself." She reaches for my hand, all lady-like, and jumps down.

"What do I need to forgive myself for?"

"Has it occurred to you that you can't forgive yourself for being ambivalent because that makes you like her?"

Is Eartha spying on my therapy?

Of course she is.

Eartha walks over to the grill. "You've had a tiny glimpse into what it's like to have a baby, a surprise baby, that isn't coming along at exactly the right time for you."

My fingers get caught in a snarl in the wig and I yank them free. "Don't you dare compare my...my....unsettledness," I think that's the word Doctor LaPointe used, "to my mother's drunken neglect."

"I didn't say they're the same," she said, staring at me for a moment. "I just said you are having a hint of what it's like to be pregnant when you don't want to be."

"I am surprised. Shocked. Maybe a little confused. But if I am able to have this baby, I will love it."

"So did your mother. She did love you. But she started

in a different place. She was a lot younger, she didn't have a man—"

"Oh, poor her that she didn't have a man. I never had a father. And that was her doing, not mine."

She sits on the rail and peels off her riding gloves. "How come you don't hate your father?"

"I don't even know who he is," I answer quickly.

"You've carried all this anger for your mother. How come it hasn't extended to your father?" She holds her hands near the fire to warm them.

"Maybe I just figured I had my hands full with my mother." I add a few more kindling sticks to the fire.

"You asked when you were little," she says.

"Exactly. And she wouldn't tell me, so I had to let it go."

"But she did tell you."

She stares at me hard and I know I'm walking on thin ice. The kind where you should not go any further, but you can't stand still either. Not when you're in the middle of the pond and the ice is splintering all around you. "She was drunk," I whisper.

"Everyone knows liquor is a wonderful truth serum."

"She told me a million things. He was a soldier. An astronaut. That he died a hero saving some woman in the city who was being attacked."

Eartha sits very still. "She also told you he raped her."

Crack. I can feel the ice splitting and me plunging into the freezing water. "Why would you believe that story?" I whisper.

"For the same reason you believed it."

The smoke from the fire is burning my eyes. "I didn't believe it!"

"Then why did you stop asking. You never asked about

him after that day."

"Because I knew she wasn't going to give me the truth."

"Or is it because you knew she already had?"

"Don't you dare try to make me feel for her! We have no reason to believe that story over all the others."

"Didn't you ever wonder where she got the money to buy the bar?"

I shake my head. Of course I wondered.

"His family paid her off."

"How do you know? You don't know anything I don't know."

"You're right. That's how you know what I'm saying is true. You just don't want to admit it because—"

"Because nothing. It changes nothing."

She smiles sadly. "She wasn't an alcoholic before she was working until two in the morning at a bar, and trying to raise a baby..."

"You could put me in a bar, without a husband, and a baby and I wouldn't turn into an alcoholic."

"Maybe. And if you put her in a marriage, with a husband, and a baby, maybe she wouldn't start hearing voices like you are." She leans toward me.

"I couldn't be more different. I am nothing like her."

"Your mother lives in your DNA whether you like it or not. As long as you fight that part of you, you're denying your inner child. And that pun is definitely intended."

I can't believe Eartha is being so mean. "I didn't invite you to this ceremony."

"Hon, I think that's part of the problem. You haven't invited me to anything in a long time."

I toss the wig on the fire and watch the flames catch. "I thought you'd be glad I'm letting go of my anger."

"I would be," she says softly. "If you really were."

Eleven

Jodi

It's late Friday night. Sofia is sleeping over a friend's house and I'm not sure when Bob will be home, so I throw on one of his old t-shirts and a comfy robe and slippers. I'm in the kitchen, making another peanut butter and banana sandwich. I've just taken my first bite when Bob comes running in from the garage. "I've got great news," he says, a big grin on his face. He pulls an envelope out of his jacket pocket like he's a magician pulling a rabbit out of a hat.

"I talked to my boss and they're going to let me go to Japan a week early. So I bought two first-class tickets for my favorite girls!"

"Bob—"

He hugs me then pulls away. "I know normally we wouldn't take Sofia out of school for a vacation but this is a chance of a lifetime."

"Bob—"

"I texted her and she's e-mailing her teachers so they can put her work together. She's only going to miss five days of school ."

He's already told Sofia. Great. I put my sandwich down, having lost my appetite.

"And she promised she'd get most of it done on the flight over."

He sits at the breakfast bar, spreading out the folded papers he's pulled out of his briefcase. A color-coded, travel itinerary. I haven't seen him this excited since...well, in a long time. I find it ironic, the bad kind of irony, that I'm going to pop his happy balloon by killing the proverbial rabbit. "I can't travel."

He doesn't even look up. "Of course you can."

"No," I say, "I really can't." This isn't how I wanted to tell him.

"Why the hell not?" He gets up and paces, which really consists of turning around and around in the confined kitchen. He's making me dizzy.

"I should have known," he mumbles. "You acted all upset that I was going without you. No matter what I do."

"I'm pregnant." I wanted to say we're pregnant. I know it's politically correct. But politics aside, I'm pregnant. He isn't.

Now he looks at me. "Jodi, that's not funny."

I walk around and sit on a stool and face him. "I'm not kidding."

"What do you mean?"

"I'm pregnant. We're probably going to have a baby."

"I don't understand," he says, sitting on the matching stool and spinning to face me. "I didn't think it was possible—"

"I'm forty. Not dead."

"It's almost indecent," he mumbles. At the look on my face, he quickly adds, "I don't mean you. I'm five years older than you. I'll be fifty before the kid even goes to kindergarten."

"I thought you'd be happy." It had never occurred to me, not for one single second, that Bob wouldn't be thrilled. I had honestly thought it was okay that I was floundering in this storm because I was so sure he'd steady our boat. "I thought you wanted another baby," I say, turning on my stool so we aren't facing each other.

"I did," he says quietly.

"You don't now?"

"Well, I'm not going to say that if you are pregnant."

"Since when is unprotected sex safe?"

"With our history, I just thought…you know, we were past all that."

"Right. Cuz I'm a relic. A fossil who couldn't possibly get pregnant." It never occurred to me he would think all the same things I had thought. We never think alike.

"I know you've wanted a baby forever—" he says.

"Did you know if you are pregnant after thirty-five, they call it a geriatric pregnancy. Over forty must be post-geriatric." I remember wanting to be pregnant. Not a medical condition. Over the years, a hard outer shell has entombed my body, meant to protect me from the pain of not getting what I wanted. I didn't realize I would also be imprisoned by my own shell. Now I don't know what I want. But I thought I knew what *he* wanted.

He reaches out and holds my hand on the breakfast bar. The granite is cold and hard under our hands. "I'm sorry," he says, clearing his throat. "I'm trying to wrap my head around this. I just thought that since it didn't happen all those years we were trying—"

I finish the sentence for him, "That I couldn't get pregnant." When he looks at me does he see a raisin of a woman, making sex with me completely safe? A raisin so old that I can't become a juicy grape again even if you soak me in wine for a thousand years, so a little semen certainly isn't going to plump me back up. I wrap my arms around me, feeling ugly inside and out. "My hormones are off again, so there are no guarantees."

He shakes his head sadly. "There never are." He takes a deep breath and puts on a good face. Trying to rebound. Searching for the right thing to say. I know because I do it all the time.

"I can try to postpone my trip," he says slowly.

I know he's trying to say the right thing so I say the right thing back. "You don't have to postpone your trip."

"Jodi, you don't handle these things well."

"You're right. I never did. But this time is different."

"You say that every time, that this time things will be fine." He sighs and one of the papers flutters to the ground. "I'll just postpone Japan until this is over."

I pull my hand out of his and get up. "This? Over?" I'll admit to being surprised I'm pregnant. And shocked. I'll even admit to being ambivalent. But I will not admit to just waiting for it to be over. I toss my uneaten sandwich in the trash.

"Jodi, calm down."

"Why should I calm down? I just told my husband of eighteen years that we're going to have a baby, and all he can think is he should postpone his trip until I lose the baby." I am getting perverse pleasure out of hearing him say all the horrible things I have been thinking. When he says them, I can argue. I can fight.

"Japan is a big deal," he says.

"I know it is. I'm not denying that. But this is a big deal, too."

"Jodi. You know the odds aren't good."

"What if the baby can hear you? What if the baby can hear you saying how you don't want him or her?" It's one thing if one parent is unsure, but this baby needs someone on his team. Someone who wants him or her. I put a protective hand over my belly the way women have been doing since the beginning of time. "I am pregnant," I say. "With a baby. Our baby. And there's a very good chance, in seven months, we'll be bringing this baby home."

He reaches for me but I step back.

"Oh, Jodi," he says. In those two words I hear sympathy, and regret...and pity.

He feels sorry for me.

"Jodi," he calls again and I turn around. He points down at the floor. His face is so pale I look down. On the inside of my right knee, a thin river of blood is running down my leg.

I lift my robe stare at the bright red slash on the inside of my thigh. It looks like the minus sign I had expected to see on the pregnancy test a few days ago. I feel light-headed. Not my blood. Not my leg.

I have no power. No power of getting pregnant, of staying pregnant, of miscarrying. I was pregnant. And now I'm not. In this moment of complete powerlessness, I find a kernel of acceptance and I cling to it. It doesn't matter what I am, or what I do, or what I feel, because I am not the rudder of the boat. I am simply a sailor fighting the winds. I let go of my toothpick of an oar because the tides of the universe are deciding.

Bob grabs me because my body has lost the core that holds it up. Suddenly, I go from feeling very light to very heavy. When he catches me, my protective shell cracks and repressed feelings pound through my heavy veins. My understanding of what it means to be a a mother, once so clearly defined, is in chaos.

Bob picks me up in his arms and carries me into the downstairs bathroom. He turns the shower on and steps into the shower, never letting me go. The hot water runs over both of us.

"Can you stand up?" he asks.

I nod and he gently puts me down. He bends over and washes the blood off my legs. I stare down at him, this man I've been married to forever. The airline tickets are soggy and drooping over the side of his pocket. Waves of feeling, each different than the next, crash over me, pounding me. I don't have the strength to outrun them. Or resist them. So I feel them. For someone who hasn't known how she feels in a very long time, every emotion is shocking to my system. One wave of feeling after another smashes into me. "Do you think baby knew we weren't ecstatic?" I whisper.

He stands up and takes my face in his hands. "If it worked that way, the other pregnancies never would have ended."

Tears burn my face.

"I'm sorry my reaction was so wrong," he says.

"Yeah, well my reaction wasn't what I expected either."

He stands up, still holding me. "If this is what you want, we can try again."

"I thought it was what I wanted. I mean, I remember wanting it more than anything." I try to breathe around the lump in my throat. "And I thought it was still what you wanted. I really thought you felt robbed. I know you hoped to have a son someday."

"I never felt robbed. If we did have a baby, we would have loved it...."

"But?"

"Hon, if you were pregnant, I guess that could be great, but to be perfectly honest, having a baby now, at my age, is not how I see our life going."

I lean against the wall, my shuddering breaths shaking both of us. "I guess I can let go of the guilt then."

"It was never your fault," he begs. "Jodi, you've never had anything to feel guilty about."

It didn't matter how many times he told me, how many times the doctor told me, it wasn't my fault. Deep in my heart, I always thought it was.

Bob pushes aside the curtain and wraps me in a towel. He sits down on the edge of the tub, holding me on his lap. "I have never wished for something we don't have. I'm just saying...."

Ninety percent of the time, he doesn't finish this sentence.

"...I love you," he whispers in my ear. "I always have."

When it really counts, he says exactly what I want to hear.

I know his legs have to be hurting. And his back. I also know he'll hold me as long as I need him to. Unfortunately for him, that's probably going to be a very long time. I can't think of a single reason to ever get out of the cocoon of his embrace.

My cell phone sings...*You and me against the world...* Sofia's ringtone.

Except that.

Chapter Twelve

Jodi

"You don't have to answer it," Bob says, even while he's getting out of the shower to get my phone off the kitchen counter.

"It's Sofia," I say, as if that explains everything. "And it's late." I turn the water off and take the phone from him. "Hi," I am surprised I sound so normal.

"Mom?"

Just one word from my little girl and I know something is wrong. My maternal instincts kick into high gear. "What's the matter?"

"Mom, you always said if I wanted to come home, you'd pick me up, no questions asked, right?"

I'm already out of the shower, peeling off my wet robe. "Yes, of course."

"Mom," she says quietly. "I want to come home."

"I'll be right there," I say, that intangible cord that never gets cuts pulling me toward her like gravity. "You're at Meghan's, right?" I'd prefer not to even bother with clothes, just race down to my car, a warrior ready to go to battle for my child, but I know she'll kill me if I show up naked.

"Kayla is with me," she says. "Can she sleep over our house?"

"Of course."

Bob comes back into the bathroom, sweatpants and a dry t-shirt in his hands and I start putting them on.

"Hon, what are you doing?" he asks behind me.

"Sofia wants to come home."

"Okay, but—"

"She said no questions asked," I explain.

"I hear Dad," Sofia says on the phone. "Maybe it would be better if he came."

Better for who? "I'll be there in five minutes."

"Mom," Sofia says. "Everything is okay. I just want to come home."

"You're sure you're all right?"

"Mom. I'm fine. I just want to come home."

Okay. Maybe a little breath. Probably safer to drive if I am breathing. I hang up and grab my keys off the counter.

"Jodi, I'll get her," he says, taking the keys out of my hand. "Hon, you're bleeding."

Oh right. "Fine. You drive. But I'm coming with you."

As we drive over to Meghan's house, Sofia's voice echoes around the quiet car. "I just want to come home." How many times had I gotten that call late at night when she was little? During the day, she loved the idea of a sleep-over. But usually around ten o'clock, we'd get the call that she wanted to come home. Inevitably, it would be at the most awkward time. Bob and I would have just gone to bed, joking that we could make as much noise as we wanted, and the phone would ring. I'd pretend to be irritated and throw my pajamas back on and drive to wherever she was. When she'd get in the car, though, with her teddy bear clutched on her lap and her sleepy eyes held open with sheer determination until she was home in her own bed, my world always felt right.

This wasn't one of those phone calls.

As soon as we pull in the driveway, Sofia and Kayla come out the side door and get into the car. I turn around in my seat and stare into the dark back-seat. "What's wrong? What happened?"

Two sets of teenage eyes stare back at me. "Nothing," Sofia says, some of her usual teenage bravado is back. That's a good sign, but it's also making it harder for me to read her.

"We just wanted to come home," she says. Both girls shove their overnight bag on the floor so they have more room.

"Something must have happened that made you want to come home," I continue.

"Mom," she says as if I'm the drama queen. "It's not even midnight."

For once, the sarcasm doesn't bother me. I know it's designed to distract me. "*Nothing* changed your plans to sleep over?"

Bob squeezes my hand.

"Was there alcohol?" I ask, ignoring Bob's pressure.

"Mom, please. You said no questions."

Bingo. Alcohol.

Bob squeezes my hand harder. "We promised no questions," he says softly.

I turn and study my daughter's eyes, eyes I know better than my own. I know the signs of drinking...bloodshot eyes, slack facial muscles. And honestly, I see nothing in my daughter's face that would indicate she had been drinking.

And Kayla? She's not looking me in the eye but what fifteen year old does? It's hard for me to look at anything other than my daughter, searching for signs of trouble. Searching for signs of hurt. Searching for signs of anything I need to fix.

The car has barely come to a stop in our driveway when the two of them have already grabbed their bags and are headed upstairs. "Sofia," I call.

Reluctantly, she turns around.

"Kayla needs to call her mother and let her know she's spending the night here instead."

"Mom. It's almost midnight."

Suddenly, almost midnight is late.

"Kayla stays here all the time," she whines.

"And I'm sure her mother will be fine with it. But she needs to know the plans changed."

"Mooommm," she draws that one syllable out for three full seconds. For once, her whining comforts me. It feels so normal.

"Is it okay if I just text her?" Kayla asks.

Both girls look at me for approval and I nod. They start going up the stairs. I can't stop myself. "Honey, I'm proud of you." Proud of what, I have no idea. Just proud that she was smart enough to avoid whatever it is and come home.

She stops and turns around. "Mom, thank you for coming to get us. And for trying your best not to ask questions." She comes down the few stairs separating us, into my arms. She lets me hold her for a few seconds. "We're both fine," she whispers into my hair. I wonder if she means her and Kayla? Or me and her? She gives me one more quick squeeze and runs upstairs.

I let her go. Because I have to. I managed to come to her rescue tonight and I guess that has to be enough. But from what? And how can I protect her from it again when I'm not even sure what it is?

Bob comes up behind me. "Here," he says, handing me a glass of wine. "I think you need this."

For one second, I think I can't have it. Then I remember there's no reason not to. I take a sip. Than another. "No questions asked," I mumble. "That's the dumbest thing I ever heard. Must have been your idea," I tease.

Bob holds my hand as we sit on the couch. "Actually, it was yours."

"Guess I'm the cool parent then."

He smiles. "So when it was my idea, it was dumb, and when it's your idea, it's cool?"

"It's both," I concede. "Cool for her. Dumb for us. Maybe we need to ask questions. Maybe we need to know. How do we know we're doing the right thing?"

"She's home. She's fine. She's smart enough to call us when she needs us. Sounds right to me."

"What if it's worse next time?" I ask, not ready to let it go.

"Guess we should consider ourselves lucky that she's having this practice."

"Practice? How do we know there weren't drugs? And boys on drugs? How do we know we weren't seconds away from one of the boys slipping her a date rape drug and she wouldn't have been able to call—"

"Jodi,"

"You don't know."

"She wasn't traumatized tonight. You talked to her long enough to know that. She was uncomfortable. Something was off, but she wasn't in danger."

"Maybe not this time," I mumble.

"Hon, you think maybe you're using this to distract yourself? Maybe you're projecting your trauma onto her?"

That hits close to home.

“Do we need to do anything for you? Should I take you to the hospital?”

“No way in hell I am leaving the only daughter I do have who called to come home. I’m staying right here.” I sigh. “We know how this goes. I’ll call doctor in the morning, but there’s nothing we can do.”

He looks at me. I look at him. “Let’s go to bed.”

Within twenty minutes, Bob is lightly snoring. It’s the first night in months the Japanese tapes aren’t filling our room.

I roll over, trying to get more comfortable but the silence of the night is too loud and I get up and go peak into Sofia’s room. Both girls are sound asleep. I don’t think they were drinking, but I go in and lean over to smell her breath just to be sure. Sofia smells just like she always does.

A couple of years ago I saw a show where they interviewed a woman whose two year old son had been kidnapped and found eleven years later. During the interview, the mother admitted she was afraid she wouldn’t know her own child because for years she had seen her baby in every child she saw. In the grocery store. At the park. At school. She’d see a child that was her son’s age and she’d swear that child had his eyes. Another child had his hair. One time she saw a little boy who had a birthmark behind his knee and she had sworn that had to be her own child, even though the child was of another ethnicity. When she finally was reunited with her son, she smelled him and knew he was hers.

In a court of law, I’d trust my smell of Sofia more than I’d trust a DNA test.

Eartha tip-toes into the room behind me. “Now that’s the way to sleep,” she says.

“What do you mean?”

"With that wild abandon. Long limbs going every which way. Arms flung wide open."

"When Sofia was little," I say, "she liked to be swaddled up nice and tight."

"Things change," she says, taking my arm and leading me back into the hallway. "So how are you feeling?"

"If you're my heart, why don't you tell me?"

"I am just a physical manifestation of your heart so that you can have a conversation, a connection, to your own heart. I am not here to spoon-feed your feelings to you. You've got to be brave enough to face them."

"Why would I want to do that?" I whisper. "If you don't feel something, it can't hurt you."

She smiles. "You wish that were true."

I look at my little girl, sleeping safely in her room. I think of the baby I almost had, the tiny hint of possibility that has already gone back to heaven.

"Letting go is one of the hardest parts of being a woman," Eartha says softly. "We do it with our bodies every month. We do it with our children. From the moment they are born. First we let them out of the safety of our body. Then we let them walk. And soon enough, we have to let them walk away."

I pull Sofia's door partway closed, leaving it open a crack, and lean my head against the door jam. "With the constant practice of letting go, you'd think I'd be better at it," I whisper into the dark.

Chapter Thirteen

Mel

I stand at the stove, waiting for the water to boil in my polka dotted tea kettle that has the words "whistle while you work" imprinted on the cover. Some people meditate. Sitting still, with nothing to do but hear my own thoughts, would literally drive me to drink.

Instead, I draw.

I have a desk I found on the side of the road and brought home. I painted it a vintage white and distressed it. With a pink velvet swivel chair, it is fit for a princess. Or a Queen that hasn't quite grown up, as I prefer to think of myself.

I sit down and turn the hourglass timer over. One hour. I'm a stickler for setting timers. Gives me a feeling of control. I can't control how productive I'll be but I can control how long I sit. Sometimes I sit here for a long time without even picking up a pencil. Often times I cry. Sometimes I know why.

Most times I don't.

I believe drawing has saved my sanity so I never go more than a couple of days without sitting here. My sanity was too hard earned to risk losing. This time is penance, confession, and meditation all rolled in one.

Time is the word floating around in my head today. Desperate to go back. Afraid to go ahead. Lonely time so different than alone time.

I draw a grandfather clock, simple lines curving the outline. Even with my graceful lines, it feels stern. Demanding. Reprimanding me for wasting so much time.

I crumple the paper and throw it in the Cookie Monster trash can. Every time I throw something in there he growls gleefully, "Cookie! Yum! Yum!" It makes me smile to think that even my throw-aways are worth something to someone.

Instead, I draw a grandmother clock. The shapely figure is perfect for a woman's body. I draw her a bit tilted to the side, as if she's somehow managing to rock back and forth. I draw a table with a little radio, music notes floating up from the speakers. Then I put a frilly apron on her. Her arms come out from the top of the clock, resting her hands on her curved hips. I give her little gloves with ruffles at the wrist. Big eyes and sweeping eyelashes.

I'm not sure about her hair yet. I imagine her with a classic up-do. Seems a bit too fancy. Wind blown beach hair? Too carefree. I leave the hair for now.

The actual clock, which essentially is not in the middle of her chest, I make subtly in the shape of a very round heart.

I write the question above her head..."*What time is it?*"

Instead of numbers going around the clock, I write the letters N. O. W. Coincidentally, three letters fit around the clock exactly four times, N.O.W.N.O.W.N.O.W.N.O.W, making it easy to find the answer to the question, *What time is it?*

I lean back in my chair, waiting for the sand to run out

in my own timer, wondering why now, why being present, is the hardest of all time to find?

I sit in my office and kick off my red Converse sneakers under the desk. I like to come in early, before everyone else, so that I can catch up on paperwork. Everyone thinks being your own boss is glamorous. That you can take as much vacation as you want. That you simply come in at the end of the week and collect your money.

Being the boss really means you basically have to be able to do every single job in the business because when the shit hits the fan, you are the only one still standing right in front of it. When my accountant took three months off to have a baby, every other year, I learned how to do the accounting. When the cleaning crew stole a bottle of my best gin and forgot to clean, I cleaned.

I pull out the folder with bills and write a check for the electric bill. Note to self, remind everyone to shut the lights out when they leave at night. Inevitably, if I wasn't the last one to leave, lights got left on somewhere.

I write another check to the contractor for re-finishing the wood floors.

The last check I write every month, my favorite check to write, is five hundred dollars payable to my granddaughter's college fund. My accountant had warned me that since my granddaughter was getting older, I should think about taking her name off the account. Legally, when she turns eighteen, she could take the money and run off to Europe for a couple of years instead of going to college. I explain to her that my granddaughter doesn't even know the account exists.

The last thing in the bill folder is a printout someone had given me at a meeting a few months ago. A contest for greeting cards. Sometimes, if I thought one of my drawings would help someone, I made them a card. Among friends of Bill W's, I am known as the greeting card lady. Every month, when I finish paying the bills, I come across it. Inevitably, something more important comes up and I put it back in the empty folder, promising next month I will consider it. So it is almost by habit that I only glance at it and close the folder again.

But today, sitting at my clear desk, nothing seems pressing. I grab a pencil and without even thinking, start drawing on the manilla folder. A sketch of a woman, her To Do List wrapped around her body like a mummy, from one shoulder all the way down to her ankles. One hand is on her hip and the other threads through the list wrapped around her, with a pencil ready to write the next thing that needs to be done. *Too wrapped up in my To Do List!* I take a yellow highlighter and color in the list snaking around her body, making it stand out on the black and white drawing.

I open the folder and start filling the contest application out. The first few questions are easy. Then it asks for my website. It assumes I have one.

I pick up my phone and text Jake. *Will you help me make a website?*

I put the phone in my lap, knowing he generally texts back right away. Ding. *This is the first thing you've asked me to do that didn't involve taking my clothes off.*

I laugh and type back...*If I ask you to do it naked, are you going to say no?*

Yes. Followed immediately by dots indicating he's typing...*I meant yes I'll do it, naked or otherwise.*

I smile and put the folder back in my drawer. One step at a time. When the phone rings, I answer it without even looking, assuming it's Jake calling.

"Sorry to bother you, Mel." It's not Jake. It's one of the nurses from the nursing home.

"We can't find Miss Dorothy's doll. We have looked everywhere. I remembered one time Miss Dorothy put her in your backpack when you weren't looking. Thought maybe she slipped it in when you were here yesterday."

"I'll be right over," I say, slipping my bare feet back into my red sneakers. I put the flyer back into the folder and file it away, once again glad I don't have to answer to anyone.

I park at the nursing home and open the trunk. I push aside the jumper cables still wrapped in plastic. I am convinced it's because I have them that I haven't needed them. And in the back of the trunk, four boxes of the exact same doll, all brand new. I grab one and use my teeth to break the plastic ties holding the doll secure in the cardboard box. I pour a bit of my coffee onto the doll's dress. Then roll her in the grass. I had made the mistake once of bringing a brand new doll and Miss Dorothy had screamed bloody murder that aliens had taken her baby and turned her into a doll.

I buzz the door. When the bell sounds, I take a long, deep breath and go inside. I can see Miss Dorothy in her wheelchair, beside the nursing station, where she has probably been planted ever since they discovered her baby was missing. Asking the same question over and over again, no matter how many times the nurse tried to reassure her. Even down the hall, I hear the nurse, over-worked and under-paid, assure Miss Dorothy that I have her baby and am bringing her back. Her voice is flat, having answered the same question many times.

Miss Dorothy sees me walking down the hallway. "There's my baby!" she cries, her stick-thin arms reaching out from her wheelchair. I walk faster down the hall. This has to be what mine rescuers feel like when they manage to bring a survivor up from collapsed earth. It is fun being the hero...even knowing I will soon be forgotten. I hand her the doll. The nurse and I hold our breath, waiting to see if Miss Dorothy will accept this doll as her own.

She does.

"You're a bad, bad girl," Miss Dorothy scolds the doll, even while she holds her tight.

And just like that, I go from feeling heroic to deflated. I turn and start walking back down the hall. Why can't Miss Dorothy be nice to her baby who has come back?

"Baby likes your piano playing," Miss Dorothy yells, her words echoing down the empty hall.

I turn around.

"She hopes you'll play, 'Fly Me to the Moon.'"

I can't help myself. I get drawn in. "Baby likes 'Fly Me To The Moon'?"

"It's her favorite song," she says.

"What about you, Miss Dorothy. Do you like it?" I start to take a deep breath but stop when the ammonia smell burns the back of my throat.

"When you play it I do," she says softly.

"Then *Fly Me to the Moon* it is," I say, coming back and pushing Miss Dorothy's wheelchair toward the library. Miss Edie is in there, her granddaughter sitting at a table with her. I have met her a few times and we acknowledged each other with a awkward smile. Visitors don't know anything about each other except that we are all in the same sad boat.

"Do you mind if I play softly?" I ask, not wanting to interrupt their visit.

"We'd love that, right, Gram?" Elizabeth says, clearly grateful for the distraction.

I position Miss Dorothy right beside the piano, her doll almost falling off her lap. When she doesn't have it, she raises bloody hell. As long as she has it, though, she mostly ignores it.

I start playing softly.

The music perks Miss Edie up, as it often does, and she starts talking to her granddaughter. "Did you know your mother wanted to name you Paris?"

Elizabeth holds her grandmother's hand. "She did, Gram?" she asks, although I can tell she's heard this story many times before.

"I told her no granddaughter of mine is going to be named after a city in Europe." She smiles. "So they named you Elizabeth." She smiles. "Just so happens that's my middle name."

"I know, Gram. And I love having the same name as you."

Miss Edie holds Elizabeth's hand tight on her lap. "Where's your grandfather?" she asks.

Elizabeth looks devastated. "Granddad's —,"

"Coming soon," I interrupt, wondering why family members think they have to tell the truth. I sigh and keep playing, reminding myself that everyone is just doing their best. Even when their best sucks.

"I hope he brings me a peanut butter cup," Miss Edie says.

Elizabeth, catching on, answers, "I'm sure he will,

Gram."

We can see Miss Edie's fading. The terrible disease of her mind is claiming her again, pulling her so far away that even her beloved granddaughter can't reach her. Within minutes, her jaw is slack, her eyes are glazed, and she is lost again.

Elizabeth's eyes fill with tears, the loss hurting every time. "Gram? Gram?"

I can't bear hearing her calling for her Grandmother and not getting a response so I say the first thing that comes to me. "Sometimes they're the lucky ones, because they can forget the things they wish didn't happen. The tragedy in their lives. The things they did that they can't take back."

"I miss her," Elizabeth says, taking her hand back because her Grandmother isn't holding on any longer.

"She loves you so much. That's why she tries so hard to come back when you visit." Since Miss Dorothy has dozed off as well, I tuck her doll securely on her lap. Then I stand up and pick up my purse.

Elizabeth and I start walking out together. "She tells that story every time, you know, every time she comes back to us. And it's true. My mother really did want to name me Paris."

"It's her connection to you from before you were even born."

"Gram was right...I would have hated the name Paris. It's because of her that I never let anyone shorten my name. No Liz or Beth for either one of us."

"It suits you," I say.

We get to the door with the alarm and wait for the nurse to buzz us out. When we hear the buzz, we walk out quickly, then wait on the other side for the click to let us know it is locked again.

"Coming here is so hard," Elizabeth says. "Sometimes I wish I would get locked out so I never have to come back."

I nod, understanding.

"I wonder where they go," she says. "You know, when they disappear like that."

I take a breath of fresh air. "I like to imagine their spirit isn't trapped with their body. That they get to go somewhere really good."

"That's a really beautiful thought." Elizabeth turns to me. She smiles and there is a hint of hope in it. "I imagine Gram's dancing with my grandfather. In a field of peanut butter cups." She starts walking away, then stops and turns around. "I really hope you are right."

"So do I," I whisper. I sit in my car and set the timer on my phone. I open the windows and breath deep...wishing forgetting was contagious.

Chapter Fourteen

Jodi

I sit on the edge of our bed, my suitcase open beside me, empty except for seven pairs of old lady underwear. A whole week's worth of granny panties. White, nude, and black. Sensible colors. Not a piece of lace to be found.

I had planned to splurge on my birthday and go out and buy matching bras and panties. I want to be the type of woman who wears lingerie instead of faded panties. Somehow, I just can't believe women who wear red lacy underwear forget to have sex. Women in low-rise, cotton bikini panties with pretty little flowers would consistently shave their legs and wouldn't have a dirty bathroom. A woman who wears a satin leopard bra wouldn't have a daughter who thinks she's an old lady.

That's what I had planned to do until I got derailed by a plus sign. So now here I am trying to pack for a big trip and all I have are granny panties. At least if there is an accident over the ocean that old saying, *What if you're in an accident?* won't really apply because everything will be blown to smithereens.

Then again, I think these things are indestructible. I imagine some little kid on the other side of the world finding my old panties washed up on shore. Maybe I should pack a message in a bottle wrapped in my undies for protection so that I can give the little girl who finds it some hard earned advice...never buy your first pair of granny panties because it's a slippery slope. Once you do, you're stuck with them forever.

I take a deep breath.

In the seven days since I turned forty, I found out I was pregnant. I miscarried. I picked my daughter up from her first, and hopefully last, no-questions-asked fiasco, and adopted a couple of imaginary friends.

Clearly I haven't had time to go shopping for pretty undies.

Now I have to get my family ready for a big trip out of the country. Obviously, I'm the only one who can find the passports. The suitcases. And snacks for the delays that inevitably happen on a big trip.

The dailiness of living as a wife and mother take over so much that it doesn't even seem unusual that I wouldn't have time to catch my breath. I certainly don't have the luxury of time to feel something. And I'll be honest, I'm happy to avoid. It's so much easier to take care of everyone else than to actually sit in the quicksand pit of your own feelings. It's better to just walk around it when there's so much to be done for my family.

I take another deep breath. Time for Plan B. I'll just wear all these ugly undies on our trip and throw them away at the end of each day. That way when I get home, I won't have any underwear left. Maybe the threat of having to go outside the house without any underwear on will jump-start my shopping for the pretty underwear my over forty self swore she would wear.

Eartha saunters into the bedroom and I slam my suitcase shut so she can't see inside. She walks over to my dresser and hoists herself up. "How are you feeling?" she asks softly. Slowly. As if she has all the time in the world to hear my answer.

Which is good because that's how long it would take for me to figure it out. I play with the zipper on the side of the suitcase, rolling it back and forth, the sound of the teeth biting and releasing almost hypnotic. I take a deep, shuddering breath. "I feel relief. I didn't want the miscarriage to happen, I swear I didn't. But it's like the raisinette that fell out of my easter basket and rolled under the couch. Months later, when I finally found it, there's lots of dust. Which equals guilt. When I blow that off, there is fur, which equals fear. After I peel that off, the chocolate is sadness, because this does hurt. But the raisin, the center of what I'm feeling, is relief." I breathe in again, even though I don't feel like I ever exhaled. "I wanted it for so long, I think my want just became a habit."

"What if the miscarriage was your wake-up call?" Eartha asks softly. "What if I'm here to remind you that desiring is part of what it means to be a woman?"

Desire? I don't know if I even remember the definition of desire, never mind the feeling. I stand up and go toward the closet. "I think I better finish packing," I say, hoping she'll get the hint and leave me alone.

Instead, she asks, "Are you excited about Japan?"

"Don't you know what I'm feeling?"

"Do you?" she purrs.

Who knew you could purr sarcastically?

"Let me help you," she offers, jumping off the dresser.

I cringe as I hear her lift the cover of the suitcase.

"I see you packed your unmentionables already."

"The mere fact of the name," I say, "means we're not supposed to talk about them."

"I'm hardly a stranger." She reaches into the suitcase, "May I?" she asks politely.

I nod, because what's the point.

"I just want you to say whatever adjective comes to mind."

I take a deep breath. How bad can it be?

She opens the suitcase the rest of the way and I see a jumble of panties. "Unorganized," I say. "Overall I'm pretty damn organized so I think a little rebellion is good for the soul," I say.

She bends over, her graceful hand poised over the pile of my unmentionables. She pulls out a pair. "Adjective?" she asks, "First thing you think when you see this?"

"Faded." Okay, not as cool as rebellious, but still....

She pulls out another pair. "And this one?"

"Old."

She drops it on top of the dresser and gets another pair.

"Stretched out," I say.

She drops it on top of Old and gets another.

"Worn." A pile of sad adjectives sit on top of my dress-er.

"Holey." Seriously? I have underwear that actually have holes? "Wait! In my rush, I must have grabbed my period pile."

Eartha raises one perfectly shaped eye-brow.

"You know, the old panties you keep for when you have your period," I explain.

"Considering you haven't had your period in a couple of months, I wouldn't think these would be at the front of your drawer. But okay." She turns around and moves to my dresser, clearly knowing she's only going to find more granny panty carcasses in my dresser.

I grab a used-to-be bright white granny panty and wave it, the proverbial white flag, trying to make a joke out of my surrender. "We are not all you. We can't all walk around in kitten heels, always perfumed and seductive."

She closes the drawer. "This is what you choose to put beside the most feminine part of you. Old, faded, and worn is what you have touching the most intimate part of you all day long. No wonder you never want the lights on when you're having sex. It's not about Bob. You don't want to see yourself," she says. Her heels scrape the floor as walks out, shaking her head.

I put the underwear I have wrapped around my hand back in the suitcase and close it. Even Eartha Kitt, the quintessential sex kitten, isn't up to the task of resuscitating my desire.

A few minutes later Bob comes upstairs. "Whatcha doing?" he asks.

I check to make sure the suitcase is still closed. Eartha's right. I don't want him to see my underwear, on or off me. "Packing," I try to say lightly.

He leans against the door jam, his hands shoved in his pocket. "I wanted this trip to be good for you. For us."

I know he did. All these years, he's tried to take care of us. Provided for me and Sofia. Worked hard so I didn't have to. He stayed in a job that I know isn't his passion so I could stay home and be Sofia's Mom. When was the last time I thanked him? Thanked him for taking such good care of me. Of his family. "It's very exciting," I say, knowing it's what he wants to hear. What he deserves to hear.

"The timing isn't right." He shakes his head. "Asking you to leave home right now isn't good for you, is it?"

I can exaggerate. I sometimes flex the truth. But I can't out and out lie. "I don't want Sofia to miss this. Or you. And I don't really want to miss it either...."

"But you don't want to go," he says, finishing my sentence. He sits on the bed, beside the suitcase.

There isn't room, so I sit on the other side the suitcase and take his hand over the top of it. Our fingers thread together the way they have a million times. "I'm sorry. I don't mean to sound ungrateful—"

"Jodi, you've been through a lot. We should all stay home. I can take time off—"

"If you both miss it, I'll feel too guilty. I really want you to go. You and Sofia would have a wonderful time."

He gives me a look I can't quite read. "What will you do here by yourself?" he asks.

"I'll probably nap," I say. Then sleep. Then go to bed. And buy underwear, dammit. "Nothing much," I add.

He squeezes my hand so much it hurts. "Sometimes leaving someone alone is the way you love them," he says.

It's so not like him to be this philosophical.

"I'm just saying...I don't want to leave you alone. But if leaving you alone is right for you, then I guess that's what I should do."

I don't know what to say so I just squeeze his hand tighter.

"I think the way you've wanted me to love you for a while now has been to leave you alone, but what if I'm wrong?" He looks at me intently. "Are you feeling loved?"

Am I feeling loved?

I have felt...not neglected...not ignored exactly. Just somewhat unimportant. Superfluous in my own life.

I push the granny panty filled suitcase aside and hug him, feeling his arms tight around me in a way I haven't felt in a long time. “I am now,” I whisper, grateful he has figured out a way to love me, even while I’m feeling unlovable. A way I would never have recognized as love until he told me.

Sometimes the best way to love someone is to leave them alone.

Chapter Fifteen

Jodi

In the seventeen years I've lived in this house, I don't think I have ever woken up to it completely empty.

Of course Sofia's gone to summer camp and to weekend sleep-overs, but then Bob was here. And Bob occasionally traveled for business, but then Sofia was here. Now that I think about it, I am sure this is the first time I have woken up alone in this house. Completely alone. Just me. Me and no one else.

My first morning after Bob and Sofia have left for Japan, I am not surprised I wake up at six-thirty, right on schedule. I lay very still, listening to all the things I am not hearing..."Mom, where's my...?" "Mom, you know I hate wheat toast." "Hon, I'll be late tonight."

Without my To Do list breathing down my neck, without Sofia and Bob here, I don't have to get up. And I did promised Bob I would rest.

So I roll over and listen to silence.

Or I try to listen to silence.

Then silence sounds empty to me. And I start thinking that empty isn't a sound. But I swear I can hear empty.

I pull Bob's pillow over my head. I don't like the sound of empty.

Because of course then I feel empty.

Turns out I don't like the feel of empty anymore than I like the sound of silence.

The house feels different without my family in it. Without knowing they will be home soon. Almost hollow.

Which is exactly how my body feels. Even though I hadn't felt pregnant, I still recognize this emptiness. Miscarriages often are a silent, empty loss. Often, especially if it happens early, the world didn't even know you were pregnant, so you can't even tell them about the loss. And Hallmark doesn't offer a *Sorry you miscarried* card. I know, because after my second miscarriage I looked. I had walked through the aisles of a gift shop, tears streaming down my face, looking for a card, for proof that the world recognized my loss.

No card.

Thoughts feel like tiny little bedbugs biting me so I jump out of bed.

Coffee. I get up and go straight for the hazelnut coffee. Normally I make the first pot plain and strong the way Bob likes it. Then I have to finish that pot or I feel guilty for wasting it. Then I make a small pot of hazelnut and feel guilty for drinking three cups before lunch.

Today, it's straight to hazelnut heaven.

After my first, but certainly not my last cup of coffee, I open the cabinet with three types of peanut butter—creamy for Sofia, extra nutty for Bob, and natural peanut butter for me that requires a high powered tool to mix the damn stuff. On the inside of the cabinet is a menagerie of different colored stickies. This is my Hope-To-Get-To To Do list. I take every sticky down and line them up on the kitchen counter.

"Open window and clean windowsill." Yuck. It's like an insect graveyard in there. I put that sticky back up on the inside of the cabinet.

"Clean oven." I am sure that oven cleaner stuff is cancer causing. Sticky goes back.

"Bleach recycling container." Ditto for bleach fumes.

"Take out and wash refrigerator drawers." Murphy from Murphy's law lives in my fridge. The second I clean a drawer, milk or something else equally smelly gets spilled... so why bother?

I put all the stickies back inside the closet, a rainbow of why bother that leaves me feeling exhausted, and close the cabinet so I don't have to look at them.

I go into the living room and lay on the couch. The sun pours in the window and my eyelids drift closed. Absorbing vitamin D seems like a worthwhile chore. I drift in and out of that half asleep, half awake place. Maybe that's why I only open one eyelid when I hear the front door open. An elderly, bearded man dressed in a robe comes walking in my front door. I would be afraid if it wasn't for the long wings cascading down his back. The door is locked, I know I locked it last night, but maybe that's what the long pole with the curved knife on the end is for. Picking locks.

Seems I have another new friend. "So who are you?"

"The scythe doesn't give me away?" he asks.

"I'm not even sure what a scythe is."

He holds the medieval looking weapon out in front of him.

I shake my head.

He holds out his other hand, an hourglass swinging in front of him.

I shrug my shoulder. "Still nothing."

"I'm Father Time." He sits in my rocking chair, a little dejected. I imagine he's used to a better reception.

He does seem a little more shimmery than Jack and Eartha. "You're the friendly version of the Grim Reaper," I say, wondering why he has shown up.

He rocks back and forth, looking very regal. "Most people don't know that about me."

"When I was pregnant with Sophie, I read that playing Mozart and reading Mythology was good for our baby's growing brain." I remember Bob would stop on his way home from work and get me a small bag of M&M candy. He said I was doing my M&M job, Mozart and Mythology, to make our baby smart. And it was his job to keep me happy with daily chocolate."

"Don't worry," Father Time says, interrupting my memory. "I'm not here to collect your soul."

I try to bite my tongue but I can't help myself. "So what are you here for?"

"I'm here to give you the gift of perspective."

That sounds really serious. I'm not sure I want perspective. "Why can't someone I want show up?" I ask. "I'd love to meet Oprah."

He laughs so hard he almost drops his hourglass. Somehow I think that would be really bad.

"Oprah!" he repeats. "That would be like sending a kindergartener who still picks his nose to Harvard."

I am not sure I appreciate being compared to a five year old with terrible habits. "Well, if you can take me back in time, how about you take me to Brad Pitt. Not Brad Pitt now, but Brad Pitt from Thelma and Louise. You know the scene, where he peels off that white t-shirt off his tanned chest—"

He strokes his long beard. "Why would you ask for something you don't really want?"

"Maybe it's because I don't believe you can take me back in time."

Father Time leans forward. "I love a non-believer. One of the biggest perks of my job. I had a specific time in mind for you but I could substitute. If there is another time that you really want, I'll consider it."

I see the picture of my little Sofia on the mantle, the one with her bright eyes shining above the candles on her second birthday cake. "I want her," I say, pointing to the picture.

Father Time gets up and goes over to the mantle to take a closer look. "Just curious. What do you think she can teach you?"

My stomach aches with yearning. "I just miss her."

"Mommy!"

"Did you hear that?" I whisper.

Father Time smiles, his dimples winking just above his long white beard. "Consider this a freebie," he says, walking back out the front door.

"Mommy."

That little voice, more precious to me than my own heartbeat. It's her...my little Sofia. I'd know that voice anywhere.

I race up the stairs.

The door to the guest bedroom, what used to be her nursery, is half closed, just like it used to be when she went down for her afternoon nap. I slow down as I get closer, afraid I won't see what I pray with every fiber of my being is inside. I peek around the corner.

Standing in her crib, is my baby. Her face lights up just like it did every afternoon when she woke up from her nap and I came to get her. I run inside and pick her up. She wraps her pudgy little arms around my neck. If I could die and live eternally in a moment, this would be it.

I sit in the rocking chair, holding her on my lap. She likes to cuddle for a few minutes after she wakes up. Sometimes she'll talk. Sometimes she will just sit and be quiet, with her face tucked in the crook of my neck. I often wondered if she was smelling me like I smelled her, imprinting me in her heart.

Every sense is on high alert, knowing this can't be real. And it certainly can't last. But it feels so real. The delicious weight of her body on my lap, her sweet little voice mumbling some baby talk sounds like a chorus of angels.

It could be ten minutes, or ten hours, later but she starts squirming, just a little, and I know that means she won't be happy on my lap for much longer.

Eartha leans against the door jam. "It's almost time for her to go," she says softly.

I stare at her, my arms bands of steel around my baby. "I can't let her go."

"Mommy, what's wrong?" Sofia asks.

"Nothing," I say, even though there are rivers of tears on my face. I turn to Eartha. "Please, please don't make me."

"You have to let her go," she whispers.

"I really don't think I can. It's just impossible." I hold her as tight as I can without hurting her.

Eartha points to all the pictures on the wall, a shrine to Sofia throughout the years. Sunlight dances on the glass of all the images of Sofia over all the years I have loved her. "If you don't let her go," Eartha says, nodding at the baby on my lap, "then you can never have that birthday party when she turns three." She points at another picture of Sofia in her ballet costume for her dance recital when she was seven years old. A little ladybug. "Or this little ballerina." I've been walking by that picture for so many years now, I can't remember the last time I really saw it.

"And look at this cutie," Eartha says, holding a picture of eleven year old Sofia grinning from ear to ear while she rode a dolphin on a family vacation.

Eartha holds out her hand. "Why don't you come with me now?" she says to Sofia.

Sofia, always a little shy, looks up at me, waiting for permission. I can't say the words out loud, but I smile reassuringly through my tears and open my arms, letting her off my lap. She takes Eartha's hand and they walk down the stairs. The sun reflects off the glass of all the picture frames, making the air in the stairway shimmer with ghosts of Sofia's past. It's too bright and I have to close my eyes.

Chapter Sixteen

Jodi

I sit on the chair in the therapist's office, my knees touching in front of me, angled a perfect forty-five degrees to my left. My hands are folded neatly on my lap. The picture of sanity. I need to talk to someone besides figments of my imagination. Plus, I need to confess their existence and find out if I should be on medication.

Funny, when I was thirty-nine, I didn't have a therapist. Or imaginary friends.

Doctor LaPointe sits in her chair, her notebook attached to her lap like a permanent prop. "I'm glad you came back."

"I told you I would call for another appointment." Which, I'll admit, translates to...Your're damn right, I wasn't coming back.

But here I am.

Because although I thought two imaginary friends is somehow acceptable, three isn't. Everyone knows three strikes means you're crazy. "This is like confession, right?" I ask. "I mean, you're bound by law that you can't tell anyone what I say, right? Like a priest. Or a lawyer." Confidential. That's the word I was looking for.

She smiles. "Unless you tell me you're going to harm yourself, or someone else, you're safe here. And figuratively, like stating that your mother is dead on your personal forms, doesn't count."

Clearly, becoming a therapist hasn't cured her OCD.

"Last time you were here," she says, looking at her notes, "you told me you are forty, pregnant, and ambivalent."

I clench my knees a little tighter. "I don't remember agreeing to ambivalent."

She holds up her notebook. "It says it right here. We talked about you not being sure how you feel."

I nod. I want to argue there's a difference between "not sure how I feel" and "ambivalent" but what's the point? I sigh. "I miscarried five nights ago."

She puts her notebook down. "I'm sorry," she says softly.

"I am not here to talk about that."

"Why am I not surprised?" She makes a note. "Seems you come here to not talk about a lot of things."

"I have an issue and I am here to talk about it. What more do you want?"

"You have an issue besides denying your mother's very existence, and finding out you're pregnant and being unsure how you feel about that, and then miscarrying and being unsure how you feel about that?"

"Why are you so mean?" I whisper.

"I'm not trying to be mean." She leans forward. "I think you're on the edge of deciding if you're going to be honest with yourself. Life has nudged you toward the edge and I think you're doing everything you can to dance, and deny, and side-step. And I think if you manage to back away now, with all your years practicing avoidance, you may never look fully inside."

"You don't even know me," I say softly. Translation—you hit the nail on the head.

"Therapy, at least I think for you, isn't about me getting to know you. It's about you getting to know you." She pauses for a moment, obviously giving me time to let that sink in, then asks. "So what is this other issue you do want to talk about?"

"Eartha Kitt. Jack Nicholson. And Father Time."

"What about them?" she asks.

"They've been showing up."

"Showing up? Showing up how?"

"Well, when I took the pregnancy test, Eartha suddenly appeared in my upstairs bathroom. And when I got home the other day, Jack did a little jig on my dining room table. And then this morning, Father Time stopped by."

"And what are they all doing?"

"Talk, talk, talk. They're worse than you. No offense. At least it's your job. They go on and on."

"About what?"

"Well, Jack talks about truth. He's always like, 'you can't handle the truth.' I know it's cliché, but essentially he's always calling me a chicken. He's annoying. And abrasive."

"And Eartha?" she asks.

"I like her better than Jack, that's for sure. But she's intimidating."

"Intimidating how?"

"She is just so sophisticated. She's got sass."

"Jodi, I certainly don't know you well but I'd say you have plenty of sass."

"I've got about as much sass as—"

She grins. "As Eartha Kitt."

I want to believe her. I want to believe she's telling me the truth and not just saying it because I'm paying her an exorbitant amount of money to be my human pretend friend instead of my imaginary friend. Then again, she never says what I want to hear so maybe she does mean it. "Maybe I used to have sass, somewhere, buried under layers of…I don't know…something."

"Do you think these people are real?" she asks casually.

I stare at her. "Jack Nicholson, the actor, is very real. The Jack that's at my house isn't real. I know that." Mostly, ninety-nine percent, I know that. "I see them, but I don't see them like I see you. I'm not confused about what is real and what isn't."

"Some people meditate. Some people journal to find themselves. There isn't one right way to do it." She pauses again. "So why do you think you're seeing these people?"

Honestly, I haven't even thought about it. "I think they're like imaginary friends."

"And why do you think you would you develop imaginary friends on your fortieth birthday?"

"Because I'm lonely?" I answer as a question, knowing it's the truth.

"Seems your psyche has come up with a very unique and interesting way for you to talk to yourself."

"So you think they're parts of me?" I ask, not admitting that is what I secretly hoped was happening.

"What do you think?"

I lean back in my chair. "I wish I was that cool."

"You said earlier your sass was buried under layers. Layers of what?" she asks.

"Life. Just layers and layers of life."

"Sounds like your sass, your inner Eartha, is ready to

come out." Her pencil is still and she's smiling. She's quite pretty when she smiles.

"I'm afraid," I admit.

"Of what?"

"I'm afraid if I uncover myself my sass or whatever you want to call it, nothing will be there. It's so much safer to have a big mound of doo-doo, knowing at some point there was buried treasure in there. At least there's the hope it's still there. But if you wash it off you might find that the acid, or the maggots, ate all the treasure and now you've got nothing left."

"So you're afraid there's no real you left inside of yourself?"

I lean back in the daisy chair and look at the ceiling. "I thought if I had the family I didn't have, then everything would be all right."

"What would be all right?"

"Everything."

"Be more specific."

"I would be all right. I got the family. And for a while, everything was right. And then slowly it wasn't. Even though it was. Even though everything is. My life is fine. I am fine. I'm just...."

"Just what?"

"Disappointed. I thought everything would be better than fine. For a little while, I had the American dream in my grip. For a couple years, when Sofia was young, and Bob and I were new parents. We'd just bought the house. I had it all. Everything I wanted. Everything I didn't have before. It was heaven. And it's been slowly eroding ever since. Slowly, so slowly that for years I couldn't even see the difference. I feel like I fell down the rabbit hole of middle age where everything that mattered is gone. Or going. And I'm afraid to let go of the little bit that's still there because what's going to be left?"

"Maybe something new is there," she offers hopefully.

"I don't want new."

"Apparently you wanted new friends."

I laugh. "Guess I did."

"Why not hear what they have to say?" she asks.

"I have been listening."

"Have you really? Just listened. With no judgement?" She leans forward, a few stray curls falling over her eyes. "Just go home and ask them what they want. Ask them what they are trying to tell you."

"So it's official? You're professionally declaring I'm not crazy for having imaginary friends?"

"You're not crazy for having them," she says, making a quick note on her pad and ripping off the page and passing it to me. "But you would be crazy if you didn't engage with them."

I look down at the piece of paper. It looks like a prescription, complete with a big Rx in the corner, and reads...

Doctor's Orders. Take one imaginary Advil, have a real conversation with a couple of self-proclaimed experts, and call me in the morning.

Chapter Seventeen

Jodi

On the drive home I convince myself that this morning was just a dream. But as soon as I get home, I go straight for the stairs. I couldn't stop myself from going to the guest bedroom if the house was on fire. Even though I know it will be empty.

And it is.

I wish the cushions on the rocking chair were still the faded pink color from being washed so many times. When Sofia moved into the bigger bedroom and I turned this into a guest room, I recovered the cushions with burgundy material. How could I have ever thought that was a good idea?

Time has passed in the blink of an eye. I haven't changed. I haven't caught up. The ride of life is going faster and faster. It's like I got off to go to the bathroom, I swear I was only gone five minutes, and five years have passed. I say that I'm trying to catch up, that I need to catch up, but that's not true.

I want to stay there.

For a few brief years, I was living in my own personal Happily-Ever-After. All of my life, I just wanted a happy family. And when Sofia was my little angel and I was her Mommy, I was happy.

But the story kept going, right past my Happily-Ever-After.

And as much as I spent my young life trying to run toward my Happily-Ever-After, I've spent my adult life trying to run back to it.

I look around the extra bedroom with its perfect bed set and matching bed skirt and curtains. You won't find a bed-skirt on any other bed in the house. This room is the nicest in the house. It reminds me of a game I played when I was little...which of these things doesn't belong? An apple, an orange, a banana...and an ice pick.

And it hits me—this room is overcompensating for not being turned into a nursery again.

I start to cry.

I walk down the hall to my bedroom and it's like there is a solid wall of pain instead of a door and I can't even walk in. Sex. How many times did I say yes because it was easier? How many times did I insist on having sex because it was the right time of the month? How many times did I say yes because it made me comfortable that we were having sex the "right" amount of times for a happy marriage? And how many times did I say no, not because I wanted to say no, but because I wanted to punish him for something? When was the last time I said yes just because I wanted to? When was the last time I said no because that's what I really wanted to say?

I go downstairs, feeling years of pent up tears erupting from the bottom of my soul. I walk into the bathroom for some tissues. I can still see the blood spiraling down the drain of the shower. This time Bob isn't here to hold me. It's like a damn has broken inside me and I sit on the edge of the tub. How do I grieve what never was?

"You should be an expert at that," Jack says behind me.

"Do you mind?" I ask. "I'd like a little privacy."

He shivers. "I'll leave if you're planning on getting naked."

I can tell he's getting ready to deliver one of his lines.

"Cuz I never seen a woman your age naked." Then he shrugs. "I always thought that was a dumb line. Naked is always good."

I know I'm supposed to talk to him, but he's clearly an idiot. "Go away," I mumble.

"You asked a question, and I'm gonna tell you the truth!"

"I never asked a question."

"Sure you did. You asked, "How do I grieve what never was?'"

"I didn't ask it out loud."

"Well, I heard ya anyway," he says in his inimitable Jack fashion. "And if practice makes perfect, then you're the Queen of Grief. Grieving what isn't. The truth is...you don't want the truth. You like your stories too much to pay any attention to the truth. You're only happy when you don't get what you want."

"What are you talking about?" I demand.

"Why can't you be more like a man. Go see your Mom and...."

Go see my Mom? Has he lost his mind?

"...punch her in the face, and be done with it? Instead you carry around this hurt. It's so tiring."

"I'm sorry I'm annoying you," I say, not meaning a word of it. "You certainly don't have to stay. Nobody invited you."

"The truth is always here. It is what it is. It's the story you put on top of things that actually hurts you." He leans against the sink. "Like why are you sitting here on the edge of the tub crying?"

"I don't know," I moan, feeling tears well back up in my throat.

"Stop being a pussy. You're the one crying. You must know why."

"I did just have a miscarriage. Isn't that enough?"

"Be honest."

"The truth is right here!" I yell at him. "I did miscarry a couple of days ago. Even you can't deny that truth."

"If you're honest, you got off easy. You didn't want to start over."

I recoil as if he slapped me.

I always knew the truth hurt.

"You're in the middle of a rip-roaring identity crisis. You were the daughter of an alcoholic and all the stories you made up around that. Then you tried being the perfect Mom to make up for what you didn't have. And sure, you did better. But is it enough? Are your holes filled? Cuz the truth is you're not a little girl anymore. And your life doesn't revolve around being a Mom. So what's left? Seems to me all you've got left is your 'poor me' stories." He sits on the toilet and leans toward me. "You had a rough childhood. No doubt about it. The way you dealt with it is by swearing to yourself you would get a do-over with your own family. Being a good 'Mom' was supposed to take care of the grief of your childhood. Now that the job of being a 'Mom' is sort of wrapping up, you have to ask yourself. Did it take care of the grief? Or did it just cover it up?"

I wrap my arms tight around myself. I don't even try to answer.

Eartha comes into the bathroom and starts rubbing my back. Just like I do whenever Sofia throws up. "Jack, don't you think you're being a little rough on her?"

"Maybe I'm the only one willing to say it, but the miscarriage was the best thing for everyone involved."

Why does he keep saying that? And it kills me, but I can't argue with him because I think he's right. I hate that he's right. I hate that it's the truth. But there it is. I feel so guilty I taste metal in mouth.

"That may be true," Eartha says, "but it's still sad. And it still hurts."

Is it really okay that it hurts? Even though I wasn't sure I wanted a baby now? Can both things be true? That I didn't want to be pregnant *and* I can still feel this sadness burrowed deep in my bones?

She sits on the edge of the tub beside me and puts an arm around my shoulders, pulling me tight against her. "How are you doing?" Eartha asks.

The gentleness of her voice, the maternal question, breaks me down. "I feel robbed. Not robbed of a baby exactly, because I don't think I ever really believed that was going to happen. Robbed of hope. It's like I'm an astronaut and I got separated from the spaceship. Untethered. And I've got this air hose that is connected to my helmet that is supposed to give me oxygen, but now the other end is disconnected and floating around uselessly in space." I take a unsteady breath. "I feel lost," I whisper. "And alone."

"I know you don't want to hear this," Eartha says, "but what if this pregnancy was meant to give you a glimpse into the possibility that a woman can become a mother even when it's not the right time for her?"

"Are you in cahoots with my crazy therapist? You really think this was a cosmic pregnancy meant to bring me closer to my alcoholic mother? A baby came down from heaven and lived in my uterus for a few weeks just to help me empathize with my alcoholic mother?"

"Bullshit!" Jack pipes in. "She's nothing like her mother."

I'm so stunned he stuck up for me that I sit up. "Thank you, Jack."

"You couldn't find a good drink around here if you were dying of thirst." Then he adds, "Although maybe you only have girly alcohol like Kahlua™ and schnapps because you're afraid that you're just like her...afraid you'll hit the sauce?"

"Are you crazy? Eartha thinks I'm like her because I was pregnant for two days and unsettled. And you think I'm like her because I don't have alcohol in my house."

"I'm not saying you are like her," Eartha says. "But I am saying you can't move forward, really move forward, while you're so stuck in the past. Jodi, you thought you still wanted a baby."

I look to them both, desperate for an answer. "When did that change? And why didn't I know?"

Jack shrugs his shoulders and lets Eartha answer. "It's a process," she says. "Like raising a child. You've learned having a teenager is very different than a toddler. You still love her, even though she's changed."

"I like being the mom of a toddler better," I confess. "It was so much easier to love the little girl who loved me back."

"Sofia still loves you," Eartha says.

"It's hard to see that. Every once in a while I recognize my daughter in those blue eyes. And when that happens, it's like the clouds have parted and sunshine is IV'ed right into my bloodstream. Most of the time, though, it's like she doesn't even like me anymore." I take a quivering breath.

"Sometimes, when she looks at me, I swear she's plotting, counting the days until...."

"Until what?" Eartha prompts.

"Until she never has to see me again," I whisper, afraid even saying the words out loud might make it real.

"Why do you think you're afraid of that?"

Jack shifts from foot to foot, as if he can hardly stop from shouting the answer out, but Eartha gives him a look and he holds his tongue.

"I never thought that when she was younger. I thought she was going to grow up and we were going to be the best of friends."

"That still may happen."

"Not if she hates me."

Eartha stands up, cocks her neck back, and looks at me with a perfect imitation of Sofia. "Mom," she says, with the same mist of disdain in her voice that Sofia has ninety percent of the time. "You need to let your bangs grow."

Without thinking, without even missing a beat, I start defending myself. "I don't like my bangs hanging in my eyes."

"It's the style now," Eartha/Sofia says. "You'd look so much better." Her words are positive but all I hear is...*you don't look good now.* And...*you're so out of fashion.* And...*I am so much cooler than you that I get to sit at the back of the bus and you're stuck, by yourself, in the front seat, and I could never, ever talk to you in public while you wear your hair like that.*

Eartha leans towards me. "Know what she's really saying?" she asks.

I shake my head.

"She's really sayin: 'I'm fifteen and I have loved you more than anyone in the whole world. And in three years I'm supposed to leave you, and live without you, and I have no idea how I can possibly do that. But no one is asking me if I want to go off to college. Apparently I'm being pushed out of the nest, ready or not, so I hate you. Even though I love you.'"

"That's exactly how it feels! Like she's on this maniacal see-saw of emotions."

"Because she is."

I take a deep breath, afraid this mirage of understanding could disappear. "Really? She doesn't hate me?"

Eartha smiles. "Of course not."

"I miss her so much it hurts," I say. "I miss loving with abandon."

Jack can't hold himself back anymore. "You stopped loving like that when you got afraid you'd get hurt. Let me tell you something. Love hurts. That's a fact. And the more you love someone, the more they can hurt you."

"I don't know what love is anymore. When I was little, I thought love was ignoring a person's faults. When your mother is an alcoholic, that's what you do." I sit up a bit straighter. "Then I became a parent. And found out about a whole other level of love I didn't even know existed. That real, all consuming, I'd throw myself in front of a bullet kind of love." I sigh. "Now love is messy. I love you. I don't like you. The see-saw is making me dizzy. This kind of love is exhausting. I'm worn out. And no one seems to want that all consuming kind of love anyway. But without it, what's left? Driving my kid around so much that if I got frequent flyer miles for driving, I could fly to the moon and back for free. Is this what love boils down to? Comfortable? Lucky to still like my husband...but is this love? Certainly nothing I'm going to die over. But if it's not worth dying for...is it worth living for?"

Jack stands up. "Stop being so dramatic. That's our job.

You love your daughter. You love your husband. If that's not enough for you, do something about it."

"I just wish I loved them like I used to," I say, hearing the whine in my voice and hating it.

"You loved Bob with all your heart when he was a means to your end," Jack says. " And you loved Sofia with all your heart when she adored you right back. The question is...can you love them just for being them? And not for what you need them to be?"

Eartha stands up. "And you know where you need to start...."

I stare at her. "Oh no, I don't."

"You think it's a coincidence you're afraid someday Sofia won't talk to you, just like you refuse to talk to your mother."

"But I'm not an alcoholic!"

"I don't think that's why you're really mad at her."

"Of course it is."

"It's tied to the drinking. You think if she had really loved you, you would have been enough reason to stop. You think if you had loved her more, or better, or enough, then she would have stopped drinking. And here you were, pregnant by surprise, and you were afraid the same thing would happen. You were afraid your love wouldn't be enough."

I'm used to the abrasiveness of Jack's brutal honesty, but the truth cuts even deeper coming from Eartha. I lean on the side of the tub, needing the support to stand up.

Jack pipes in again. "You're so stuck in what was, that you can't see what is. Stop holding onto this grudge. Tell her you're angry. Hit her if you have to, and then let it be over."

I point at Eartha. "You think I should go talk to her?" then I turn and point at Jack. "And you think I should punch her?"

They both nod. "We might not agree on tactics," Eartha says, "but we both think you should go and see your mother."

I stare at them both for a second, wishing I could make them disappear. "You both ask way too much of me," I say, walking out of the bathroom, somehow knowing they won't follow me.

Chapter Eighteen

Jodi

I sit in the parking lot of the Boot-Scootin-Boogie and out of habit, I pull the button to release the trunk of my car. When I hear the pop, I realize two things.

One, I don't have my disguise anymore since I burned the wig.

And two, I don't need it.

I am so nervous I'm afraid I'm going to wet my pants which is strange because my mouth is so dry my lips are stuck to my teeth. I walk in. Since it's early, there are only a few scattered customers and the bartender is drying some glasses. My mother is at the cash register in the coatroom, presumably getting it ready for another night of business.

"Hi, Mom."

She looks up, her hands freezing mid-air with stacks of bills. "Jodi," she says on a sigh, as if she's not sure it's really me. "You're here. As you."

"Who else would I be?"

She smiles and shrugs one shoulder. "Someone who likes to sit in the corner and drink a Cosmo?"

"You knew I was here before?" *And you left me alone?*

I would drive seventy-five miles to see you and when I was here within touching distance, you could ignore me?

"I figured if you wanted to talk," she says, closing the cash register, "you wouldn't be in disguise." She comes from behind the desk and for one second, I think she's going to hug me. I probably imagined it but I step back just to be safe. "Today, I think I'll have something different."

"Whatever you want," she says. "It's on the house." I follow her into the main room and climb up on a stool. She goes behind the bar, saying something softly to the bartender. He glances in my direction then heads through the saloon doors into the back, giving us some privacy.

"What'll you have?" she asks.

"How about a shot of Jack Daniels." That was my mother's drink of choice when I was growing up. My mother didn't bring men home, thank God, but Jack lived with us. Jack Daniels was my invisible, evil step-father. The one who got all her love and attention.

I'm trying to play it cool since I'm still stinging from the fact that she had always known I was here. I toss back the shot of liquid courage, cursing when it lights a fire down the back of my throat and my eyes start to water.

She pours a glass of ginger-ale and slides it across the bar to me. "I'm glad to see you're not an expert at drinking."

I take a sip of the ginger-ale.

"Jodi, I'm so glad you're here. I always loved it whenever you came in. I didn't know if you would ever actually talk to me. And I was afraid if I tried to talk to you, I'd scare you away." She steps closer, then steps back, folding her hands in front of her. I notice she is cracking her knuckles like she used to do when she was nervous.

She is so grateful, so humble, so...needy but this doesn't feel as good as I imagined. I don't want her begging.

And weak. I would have thought this is exactly how I would want our first meeting to play out. I don't. I just want...*normal.*

"Are you hungry? We have burgers. And fries. With extra ketchup, just the way you like it."

I smile. "Extra ketchup is for kids."

She cracks her knuckles again. "Of course. No extra ketchup." She pushes open the swinging doors and yells into the kitchen. "One burger. And fries." She turns back to me. "Is there anything else you want?"

Words swell in my throat and I say them out loud before I can swallow them. "Are you gonna have one with me?" We both realize this is a big step.

Her eyes fill up. "You want me to eat with you?" she asks softly, as if she can't believe she heard me correctly.

"Sure, Mom. It's not a big deal." *It's such a big deal!* I wish Jack and Eartha would pop in for a few seconds so I could brag. Eartha wanted me to talk to my mother and Jack wanted me to punch her. I came up with a much better idea—have a burger.

She opens the door to the kitchen again. "Make that two burgers. And fries."

I haven't been this close to her in fifteen years. I notice she has a bit of gray threaded through her red hair, making it lighter. I thought she would look so much older, but she looks her age. Funny, she looked this age twenty years ago, too. Guess stopping drinking is her fountain of youth.

On one hand, it's like looking at a stranger. She looks stylish in her bootcut jeans. Not the low kind, not like she's trying to look younger than she is, but like she knows what suits her, what is comfortable, and there's style in that confidence. With dusty red cowboy boots, so worn they're probably as comfortable as slippers.

On the other hand, she is my mother. The only parent I've ever known. The mother who was so far from my ideal that I created a blueprint of the perfect mother by being her opposite.

Waiting for our meal, neither of us know what to say. It's like she's so afraid to lose ground that she's frozen in place. Even the knuckle cracking has stopped.

"Do you want anything else?" she asks. "Anything at all?"

"I want..." *I want a hug. I want to curl up on your lap and bawl like a baby for a decade. I want you to stroke my hair and tell me everything is going to be all right.* "I want to learn the two-step."

"I can do that," she says, practically running around the bar, taking my hand and pulling me onto the dance floor.

I realize her touching me is not a good idea. It's too close to what I want and too many miles away from what I really want. "Maybe I should start with a line dance. I remember you were good at those." I am remembering something nice about my mother? Who am I?

She shows me a few simple steps. Heel, toe, triple left. Heel, toe, triple right. I feel like I've time traveled to a place where she's just a woman teaching me a country line dance.

The bartender waves to us that our burgers are ready so we go back to the bar. I order another shot of Jack. My mother gives it to me and pours me another glass of ginger-ale. She sits beside me, but not too close, and we eat the first meal together we've had in over fifteen years.

The bar is starting to fill up and she introduces me to everyone. I feel like I am at Cheers, where everyone knows your name. I don't know any of them, but they all seem to know me. Or know of me. They're all so happy to meet Mel's long-lost daughter. Part of me wants to tell them I wasn't lost. Then again, I wasn't found either.

So I drink another shot. And dance another dance. The bar is starting to get busy, and I can tell they need her help. I can also tell she's not leaving my side which, I'll admit, feels good. She only goes behind the bar when I promise I won't leave.

So I keep drinking. And dancing. And most of all, forgetting.

Minutes later, more likely hours, the place has mostly cleared out. The dee-jay has changed the tempo from let's-get-this-party-started dance music to a soft Vince Gill song. His voice always gets to me.

I lean across the bar and my mother comes right over. "I don't want to hate you anymore," I whisper.

She smiles and whispers back. "That's the best news I've heard in forever."

"You know what else?" I think my words are slurring a bit but I can't be sure.

"What, honey?" She said it automatically and it rings a distant bell. She used to call me honey a lot.

"I had a miscarriage last week."

She reaches for my hand. "I'm so sorry."

"You know what else?" I say, leaning back, my tongue thick in my mouth.

She shakes her head.

"I didn't want to be pregnant." I hear the words and they shock me sober. It's the first time I've admitted them to myself, never mind said them out loud. And why did I say them to her? Is it because she, the imperfect mother, can't possibly judge me? "I'll have another shot of Jack," I say.

"Maybe you've had enough," she says. "You don't want to get loaded."

Is she actually telling me I should stop drinking? Oh, the irony. "Why not? I saw how much fun it was. Saw how you'd be laughing and laughing. At nothing. A joke I could never understand. Guess what, Mom? I'm starting to get the joke." I can feel I'm getting worked up. My voice is rising and I can't, or won't, stop it. "Anything can be funny. You'd be laughing at first anyway, wouldn't you, Mom? Laughing right up until you started puking. Then you'd start crying. You'd be smiling and dancing to music I couldn't hear. Laughing at jokes I didn't understand. And then you'd be crying all over me. How you were sorry. You were always sorry."

"I'm sor—"

"Don't. Say. That." I stand up on my bar stool and grab the bottle of Jack Daniels off the shelf. "C'mon, Mom. This is kinda fun. Letting loose. Worries? What worries? Have a drink with me now that I'm old enough to have some fun with you."

"You don't want to drink anymore," she says, looking deflated. Looking afraid. We have completely switched roles. I feel like I am the one in power now. And the one out of control at the same time.

"Sure I do," I say, picking up my shot glass and waving it toward her. "C'mon, Mom. It will be just like old times. But this time I'll do the deed with you. A bonding experience. Something we can do together now."

"I don't drink anymore," she says quietly. "I told you that a long time ago."

I laugh through the sudden pain that is raging through my blood. "Yeah, right. You told me a hundred times, a thousand times when I was growing up, that you were going to stop. Stop drinking for good. That this was your last drink, your last night, the last time I'd have to clean up your vomit so I could use the bathroom before school. And it never lasted. Never. So I'm sure this time isn't any different."

She leans against the mirrored wall. I can see our reflections shadow-boxing in between bottles of booze. "Is that why you kept coming back? Waiting to see if I'd fallen off the wagon? Because I haven't—"

I throw the shot back, ignoring the fact that it's now making me sick to my stomach. I drink it in one gulp. "If you haven't yet, it's only a matter of time."

She sucks in a breath as if I've punched her. But she's willing to take it. "It's been twelve years. I've been sober twelve years, three months, and two days. This time really is different. I've tried to tell you that. Every time I get a new chip, a new year under my belt, I hope it's enough time that you'll trust me—"

"Why would I ever trust you? When I needed you, anytime I needed you, the only thing I could count on was you would let me down."

"Sometimes," she says almost desperately. "I was there sometimes."

"I've read enough books to know that what you did is almost worse than always being drunk all the time. I never knew what to expect. The only thing I knew was that a binge would happen again. A storm, always threatening on the horizon. Just a matter of time."

"I wasn't drunk every day," she says softly.

I am glad to see even she knows it's a weak defense. "That's the point," I yell. "That would have been easier. It was the not knowing day after day, every day wondering, watching the clock, knowing the later you were, the worse it would be. And then sometimes you'd come in, maybe you just stopped for gas, or stopped for something for us to eat, and the relief was almost as painful as when you stumbled up the stairs. And that's if I was lucky. I was lucky if you could still walk."

I pour myself another shot. I pick it up, then put it back on the counter and push it toward her. "Drink it," I say, deathly quiet.

Tears pour down her face. "I don't want it."

"You always wanted it. You wanted it more than anything." I stare at her, daring her to deny my words.

"Jodi, please...."

"Drink it!" I scream. "You wouldn't stop drinking for me, the least you can do is drink with me!"

She stands there, her hands trembling by her side.

I grab the glass and throw it against the wall behind her. Time slows down and I watch the glass hit the mirror. Cracks spread in the mirror. I see myself in one of the shards of mirror clinging to the wall. And I see my Mom, her face streaked with tears that I caused. Eartha shimmers in another. And Jack looks sad in one of the splinters of glass. Even Father Time is crying.

In one of the larger shards of glass, I see a memory of my mother with me, before she started drinking. I forgot I once knew her as a different mother. No wonder I miss her. And she looks a lot like me, like the mother I was with Sofia when she was young. "Why couldn't you have stopped?" I whisper.

"Jodi," she says, her voice breaking.

"Why couldn't you have stopped when I was willing to do anything to help you? When I could still forgive you?"

"I should have. I wish I could have."

The mirror has shattered into too many pieces and falls off the wall, one fragment at a time.

"Why was it only after I would have nothing to do with you that you stopped?" The ground under me breaks and I fall through. I can't bear to look at her. Or see myself in what's left of the mirror. I drop my head on the bar. "Was it because of me that you had to drink?" I whisper. "Was being my mother so terrible that you couldn't help yourself?"

Chapter Nineteen

Jodi

I wake up in my bed and the first thing I realize is I am not alone. There is noise coming from my kitchen and I smell bacon. I am ravenous and nauseous at the same time, an unusual combination. The food smells so good I'm wondering if I can eat before I get sick?

The only logical thing to do now is to pull the covers over my head and try to remember last night. I know I went to the Boot-Scootin-Boogie. And I ate with my mother. And danced. And drank.

So I danced. And I drank. And I remember talking to my mother. God, and the broken mirror. I asked her the question, the one that has been rooted in my deepest darkest corner of my heart and has been locked behind a steel trap door. Apparently Jack Daniels had the key and opened the door because I remember asking...*was it because of me that you drank?*

And the next thing I remember is throwing up.

Because of the alcohol? Or because of too much honesty?

I reach out from under the covers, grab the phone off

its cradle, and pull it under the blankets. I dial Gwen's number blindly.

"Gwen," I whisper as soon as she picks up. "You need to come get me."

"I'm on my way to yoga," she answers. "Can I get you after?"

"No, come now," I whisper.

"Where are you?"

"I'm hiding in my bed."

She laughs. "Well, roll over and hide for another hour."

"Gwen!" I say as urgently as I can in a whisper.

"What are you hiding from?" she asks.

"Someone I don't want to see is in my kitchen. I have a funny feeling, and I don't want to see who it is."

"Who's in your kitchen?" She pauses. "Oh. My. God. While the cat's away, the mice will play."

I appreciate that she pretends I might be that wild. "Be serious. I need you."

"If I come get you, will you come to yoga?" she asks.

"Seriously? You're going to bribe me?"

She laughs. "It's not like I haven't tried before."

"Yes, goddammit! Just hurry up." I hang up the phone and creep out of bed, grabbing a pair of sweatpants and a t-shirt. Two minutes later I hear the screen door off the kitchen. I hesitate at the top of the stairs.

"Hi," Gwen says, walking in my back door like she always does. "I'm Gwen. I live next door."

"My name is Amelia. I'm Jodi's mother."

"Jodi's mother?" Gwen asks, sounding so surprised I want to go down there and say, "No. Aunt Jemima's pancake-making-mother."

The stool by the breakfast bar scrapes the floor. How many times have I told Gwen, and everyone else, to pick it up to pull it out so they don't scratch the floor? And what about yoga? I thought she was in such a rush she barely had time to rescue me, never mind time for a chat.

"Smells delicious," Gwen says conversationally, like it's every day she finds my mother in my kitchen making breakfast.

"I thought Jodi might be hungry this morning"

Hungry? I'm ravenous.

"I'm making omelettes. Want one?" my mother ask.

"Sure," Gwen says.

I'm starving but I sit on the top step, a voyeur in my own house.

"How about some hot chocolate while you wait?"

"Hot chocolate sounds great."

"When Jodi was little and she didn't feel well, I'd make her my special hot chocolate."

You've got to be kidding me. Gwen is drinking my hot chocolate?

"What's so special about it?" Gwen asks.

"Well, I never told her when she was little, but I'd put a dash of butterscotch schnaaps in it. Top it with whip cream and a sprinkle of cinnamon."

You've got to be freakin' kidding me! She gave me booze?

"This is the best hot chocolate I've ever had," I hear Gwen say.

"It's the dash of Kahlua™ I found under the cabinet," my mother says.

"I would never have given Sofia alcohol when she was a baby," I mumble to myself.

"So what?" Jack says, sauntering out of the guest bedroom and sitting beside me. "Plenty of parents swear by brandy on teething gums. Does that make them the worst parents in the world?"

"Great," I mumble. "This morning just keeps getting better and better."

"Why don't you just go down there?"

"I'm not going to let my mother make me breakfast and pretend everything is normal."

"Why not? You know it's what you want."

"That's not the way life works."

He sighs as if he's disappointed in me. "It's not the way you make your life work."

"I should have known you'd be somewhere nearby. I've got a splitting headache and it's all your fault."

"Why is it my fault?" he asks.

"You told me to go see her. And you goaded me into drinking, saying I was afraid I'd be just like her so I had to drink to prove you wrong. Given all that, I don't see how it isn't your fault."

"Can I ask you something?" he asks, all serious. Jack is rarely serious. And he never asks for permission so I nod.

"Who do you think I am?"

"A bossy, selfish, creepy actor guy that is stalking my subconscious?"

He smiles. "That's one idea of me."

"You got another one?"

"I am part of you. So in a way, you're right in blaming me."

"I didn't want to go see my mother last night," I argue.

"If you didn't, then you wouldn't have."

"You and Eartha made me."

"Who drove you there? Who danced and drank?"

"If you're part of me," I say, "a part that no one would want to admit to, does that mean Eartha is part of me, too? Cuz if I get her as part of the deal, you might be worth it."

"I'm the part you wish you weren't. And Eartha's the part you wish you were." He pats my knee and gets up, wandering down the hall.

Now that he's gone, I focus on what's happening downstairs. I can hear my mother puttering around the kitchen making breakfast. The fridge opening and closing, utensils being dropped into the kitchen sink to be rinsed and put in the dishwasher later. If I could see into the future, this is just how I'd like it to be with me and Sofia. Her popping over for a spontaneous visit, sitting at the breakfast bar, while I whip up something that makes her feel special. Does Sofia have a favorite dish? Is there something I make that she will miss when she moves out?

Note to self—start making Sunday morning pancakes again so that later on there will be something that Sofia will miss.

I stand up. My mother is in my kitchen, playing Future Me and it's suddenly annoying. My mother doesn't get to play me. That mother, with a grown daughter who comes home because she misses her wonderful Mom, is me. Not her. Me!

I make a lot of noise as I come downstairs. "Sorry I'm late, Gwen," I say, coming around the corner into the kitchen. I pretend that I'm surprised my mother is even there. "Oh, hi...." I was about to say, "Hi, Mom," but I'm the only Mom that's ever been in this house and I'm not willing to relinquish my title. "Gwen and I are going to yoga," I say, grabbing my purse and a water out of the fridge. "Don't want to miss the, shit, what do they call it? "séance part." *Séance? Isn't that where you contact the dead?* "I meant corpse pose." Who knew there was so much death in yoga?

"I'll just stick around and clean up here," she says. "Then when you get back, I can take you to get your car," my mother offers.

Shit! My car. "That's all right. Gwen can drop me off to get my car after class." Before class if I'm lucky. "Just lock the door when you leave," I say, pushing Gwen out the back door.

"It was nice meeting you," Gwen grabs a big bite of her fluffy omelette.

"Hell of a rescuer you are," I mutter under my breath.

"For what it's worth," Gwen says, "corpse pose is at the end of class. Not at the beginning."

"You're going to be a corpse if we don't get going." I don't let out my breath until we are in her car.

"Was that really your Mom?" she asks, looking over her shoulder as she backs out of the driveway.

"No. She's the one I ordered from Moms-R-Us."

"Nope," she says so cheerily it's irritating. "She's definitely your Mom."

"How do you know?"

"Because she looks just like you. Well, I guess it would be more accurate to say you look like her."

I'm stunned. "You think we look alike?"

"It's not an insult. She's pretty. Much prettier than I imagined."

"Why? You thought my mother would be a dog?"

"Not a dog. Maybe a fire breathing dragon with red scales across her back."

"I never made her sound that bad," I say, leaning my head on the cool window. Wish I had thought to grab some aspirin.

"Okay," she says in a tone that says, *Oh yes you did.* "You're pretty, too, you know."

I sigh. "I never thought about it, but since I was everything she wasn't, and I knew she was pretty, I guess I just figured pretty was taken and I couldn't have it. Seemed a small price to give up for not being like her in so many other ways."

"How exactly did she end up in your kitchen on a Sunday morning making a great omelette, if that first and only bite you let me have is any indication."

"Want to go back and hang out with her?" I ask. I'm jealous. I can't believe I'm jealous.

"Don't get your panties in a wad." She stops at a red light and looks over at me. "Seriously. Why is your mother in your kitchen?"

"I went to her country and western bar last night."

"She owns a bar? That doesn't seem like a good idea. She probably drinks all her profit. Although it does explain the cool boots she was wearing."

"She's not drinking now. I guess she quit a while ago."

"Is that why she wanted to see you? Part of her making amends?"

"It wasn't her idea," I confess. "It was mine." Amends... I know it's part of the twelve steps for recovery. Yet I went to see her, does that mean I want to make amends? And what exactly are amends? I'll have to look it up later. "It wasn't her idea. It was mine."

"Jodi...."

I shake my head. "Sorry," I say to Gwen, knowing I haven't heard a word she's been saying.

"How long has it been since you've seen her?" she asks.

Of course Gwen doesn't know about my clandestine visits. "A long time," I answer, taking a long drink from my water bottle

"Why now?"

"I have no idea." Okay, that's not quite true. "A voice inside me," understatement if there ever was one, "said maybe it was time."

"How do you feel?"

I take a deep breath in, hearing my automatic response, *I have no idea,* echoing around inside my body, but I wait. Maybe I do know.

"Light," I say, the word growing from that one moment of silence in myself.

"Light?" Gwen asks.

"Light. That's how I feel. Like a boulder has been taken off my shoulders. Actually, off my chest."

"Does that mean you're going to keep seeing her?"

I shrug. "I doubt it. Why would I?"

"It sounds like you've forgiven her, or at least started to."

"Forgiven her? I don't know if that's the right word. But I don't feel mad at her anymore, either. I haven't had a mother for fifteen years, but I've carried this huge amount of anger and bitterness that just festered inside me." For the first time, I wonder if I held on to all those feelings because it was all I had left of her. "I might not have a mother now either, but the anger has been mine. And if the anger is mine, then it's mine to let go of, too."

Gwen reaches over and squeezes my hand. "And she makes great hot chocolate."

I laugh. "Yeah, well, drive slow or you might get a DUI."

"I want a pair of those red cowboy boots. You gotta admit, a woman who wears red cowboy boots can't be all that bad."

"My mother loves red shoes. Red cowboy boots. Red ballet slippers. She only wears red shoes. With everything."

"Really? Why?"

"I don't know. It's just her...thing."

"That's pretty cool."

I feel the automatic judgement crawling it's way up my throat out of habit but I force a cough, symbolically releasing it. I imagine it, my Pavlovian judgement, on the side of the road like road kill and I watch it get smaller and smaller in the rearview mirror as I leave it behind.

Why deny it?

Red shoes are pretty cool.

Chapter Twenty

Mel

I watch Jodi leave her own house to get away from me. Even people who loved yoga don't like yoga when they are hung-over. Nothing like a downward dog to remind your belly it is trying to get rid of the poison of too much alcohol.

I recognize the walk of shame. I certainly had my share of nights where I drank too much, did things I was ashamed of, and woke up with people I didn't want to see.

Last night I was able to take care of my daughter for the first time in fifteen years. I held her hair back while she was getting sick. I didn't think she would want to wake up in my house so I drove her home while she slept in the passenger seat. Last night was one of my happiest nights in a long time. I felt bad for her but, truth be told, giddy for myself. The irony is that alcohol is the bridge that caused me to be in my daughter's house this morning.

Jodi had come to the Boot-Scootin-Boogie. She talked to me. She ate with me. Then she got drunk. Made a scene and smashed my mirror.

Still, best night I could imagine. A chance for us. Underneath the anger, the shame, and all the volatile emotions, a step in the right direction. I trust the power of one step at a time. One day at a time.

I fish through my purse, pulling out the watercolor markers that are always there, and I draw. In moments like this, I don't even know what I'm going to draw. As I move the pencil, a little mermaid appears, stranded on a rock, looking longingly over her shoulder. Her baby fine black hair is blowing in the wind and I tuck a small flower behind her ear.

I carefully choose one or two items to color in. I use a vintage teal to color in her tail and I dot the flower with a super light blush marker. I pick up my pencil and write three words in tiny block letters. *I miss you.*

I pour myself another cup of coffee and study the pictures on the fridge. Somehow Jodi has turned her favorite pictures into magnets so the fridge is covered with pictures of Sofia through the years.

I wonder about Jodi's experience as a mother. Was it easy for her? Did having a partner help a lot? Did being a mother ever scare her or did it just come naturally?

My baby's baby. My daughter's daughter. Another only, female child. Sofia, my own granddaughter. Another person I've let down. Another young woman robbed of generational wisdom. Or maybe Sofia is better off, cut off from generational wounds.

I pick up my drawing and use a magnet of Sofia, probably four years old at gymnastics, her pudgy elbows and knees showing in her light blue leotard, to stick it to the fridge. I notice my mermaid looks a lot like young Sofia.

It's shocking I can miss someone I don't even know.

Chapter Twenty-One

Jodi

I follow Gwen into the yoga studio. Just like I imagined, there are soft lights around the room and new age music is playing softly. My body tenses up with the implied pressure to relax. Or maybe it's because I'm hung-over.

Gwen has her own mat but there is a pile of mats in the corner for us unprepared newbies. I spread my mat next to hers and sit on the hard floor. Why aren't these padded mats more padded? There is only one place that would be more stressful—sitting in my house with my mother and then being confined in a car with her while we drive to get my car.

My yoga mat suddenly feels more inviting. Just goes to prove that everything is relative.

I look over, surprised to see Gwen already lying on her mat. She looks so relaxed, like she's been lying there for a thousand years, without a single care or thought. My body recognizes I have never felt that...quiet.

A young woman comes into the class and welcomes us. She floats to the front of the room and gracefully sits cross-legged on her mat, her palms resting on her knees that are actually touching the floor. I expected the teacher to be a wise, older woman who radiated serenity. Instead, this woman looks like the love child of Barbie and G.I. Joe. She has the grace of a ballerina and the muscles of a ninja. "How is everyone feeling today?" she asks, her voice soft and hypnotic.

"Tired," someone says.

Amen to that.

"Sad," another voice calls out.

Ditto.

"Grateful," says a voice to my right that sounds like Gwen.

"Let's honor all of it," the teacher responds. "Let's be with tired. And sad. And grateful." She takes a deep breath. "We have a new Goddess with us today," she says. "Jodi, how are you feeling?"

Shit! I try to think of something, any word they haven't used yet. "I'm…fine." I feel everyone turn and look at me with sympathy, like fine is the dumbest thing I could have said.

"We're glad to have you join us this morning."

Yeah, right. She obviously works on commission.

"I think I'm a little angry."

Who said that? They're all looking at me. Did I say it? At least everyone is smiling at me again. Who knew anger could make friends in yoga?

The teacher gets up with easy grace and walks around the room, handing a straw to each of us. "We are going to start with breathing."

Gwen winks at me, like a straw is the magic wand that will make all of my angry disappear.

"All I want you to do is breathe in through the straw. Notice the tunnel that is created with your breathe."

I don't want to be angry anymore. I don't want to be embarrassed about the public spectacle I made of myself last night. And I certainly don't want to think about asking my mother that pathetic, desperate question. Fortunately, she never had the chance to answer because I immediately threw up. Apparently I wasn't the first one to do so because a bartender appeared, like magic, with a bucket. Mom managed to steer me into the bathroom. Then she held my hair back while I was still heaving.

"There is nothing else but your breath," the teacher says. "Inhale. Exhale. No rush. Nothing else to do."

As horrible as I felt, I also felt taken care of. I even felt...forgiven. Or maybe I was forgiving.

"One of the reasons it's so hard to be present," the teacher continues in her hypnotic voice, "is because the past feels like a gravitational pull to old hurts."

I suck another breath in through the straw and feel a tear roll down my cheek. I knew yoga would be hard.

Chapter Twenty-Two

Jodi

My mother's car is parked right beside mine in the parking lot of her bar. It's late morning so our cars are the only ones in the parking lot. I barely wait for Gwen to stop her car, keys already in hand, the remote unlocking my doors for a quick get-away.

Last night feels like a dream where I traveled to Oz and took a peek behind the proverbial curtain. I survived the tornado and now I just want to get back to Kansas.

As I pull out of the parking lot, I open the window, the fresh air helping settle my stomach. I stop behind Gwen's car at the red light. When the light turns green, I watch Gwen's tail-lights get further and further away as I sit, still stopped at the green light. The light turns red again and I wait. Turning right will take me to the highway to head home. Obviously I'm going to turn right.

Jack appears in my front seat. He has a pack of cigarettes rolled up in the sleeve of his white t-shirt. I have never seen him so young. Even attractive. "You know you want to go left."

Eartha pipes in from the back seat. "For all you know she doesn't even live there anymore. It's been fifteen years."

Turning left will take me to my mother's house. The home I grew up in. A house so small it might now be called a trendy tiny home. When the light changes to green, I turn left. Ten minutes later I pull into the driveway of the house I grew up in, my car just nosing into the driveway. If anyone sees me they will think I'm lost and turning around.

The house looks...like a house. Nothing more. Nothing less.

One thing that is changed is there are window boxes with brightly colored flowers. "Obviously someone else is living here," I say. "Flowering plants like that, even if they are in a window box, require care. And we all know she's not very good at taking care of anything." I look over my shoulder, ready to back out onto the road, but cars are coming so I have to wait.

"Or maybe," Eartha says, a soft dare, "the window boxes are proof that she has changed."

"What do you want me to do? Look in a window?"

Jack jumps out of the car. "My thoughts exactly."

"Goddammit!" I pull further down the driveway. "I hope the new owner comes out and shoots him," I mutter under my breath. I leave the car running, but I get out. As I walk up the driveway, I see a deck has been added to the side of the house. Two sliding glass doors have replaced the wall. Perfect for spying. Jack is already on the deck, his wind blown hair electric around his head, his infamous eyebrows raised in that crazy expression. As I climb the wood steps, he comes and hooks his elbow with mine, dancing me around in a do-si-do. "Great idea, great idea, great idea today," he says in a sing-song voice.

I pull my arm out from his. On the deck is one turquoise adirondack chair. Not the plastic kind you can get at any store. A real wood one. With the words *One day at a time* painted on the back of the chair. A piece of art actually. But there is something lonely about a single chair. I think of our deck with the grill. And the table with four chairs.

I tip-toe up to the sliding glass door and peak inside. Same couch. New chair. Bigger television. A pellet stove has replaced the ancient wood burning stove we used to have. God, I hated stacking the wood my mother would cut. I can't imagine Sofia stacking wood. Then again, I can't imagine myself chopping trees for heat either.

I try the door. Unlocked, as usual. Jack jumps up, practically knocking me inside the door. "You two stay out here," I say, rather harshly. "I can do this myself."

Jack shrugs and leans up against the wood railing surrounding the deck and smokes a cigarette. Eartha gives me a slight nod and sits gracefully in the chair.

I step inside. This house, the past, isn't as threatening as I remembered. The house is old. The memories are old. Maybe it is time to let all this go. All the anger and resentment. It is what it is. Was what it was.

I walk down the hall to the bedroom that used to be mine. It feels smaller, and at the same time somehow bigger, than I remembered. My window seat has been replaced by an old fashioned desk with mason jars filled with different colored markers and pencils. My room has been turned into a craft room. A regular Martha Stewart transformation. I suppose it isn't such a surprise. My mother used to help me with school projects. I swore she liked doing them better than I did, but I never complained because I liked the help. And she got me good grades. When other kids used glitter glue on their posters, my mother would use a heat gun to emboss my signs.

Is this how she unwinds after work now instead of drinking?

The closet doors have been taken off and the sunken walls are lined with display shelves. The shelves have little figures carefully displayed. A pear with a clay head. She carries a little sign that says, "I am PEAR-fect!" Another one is completely covered in buttons. Even her hands and feet are made of buttons. Wire swirls around her head with tiny buttons enmeshed in the wire curls. Her sign says, "Don't push my buttons!"

I laugh. These are adorable.

Another one, her body wrapped like a mummy in ribbon

that has the words, "To Do List", imprinted on the ribbon. Her sign said, "Too wrapped up in my To Do List!"

Another one is made of two onions. A bigger one for the body and a smaller one for her head. She has onion rings for her hands and feet. And a single tear on her cheek. "I don't know why I can't stop crying."

These little creations are starting to press on a nerve. How is it possible that my mother is tapping into my inner feelings?

The next one's body is made out of an hourglass shaped clear vase and her head is sculpted from some kind of opaque clay. Her sign reads, "When did I become invisible?"

Now they just are pissing me off. My mother has never felt invisible a day in her life. My mother is nothing like me. More importantly, I am nothing like her.

I see the last one. This one has a body made out of a cactus and her sign reads, "I just need a hug!" I smash my fist down on the cactus and the thorns pierced the side of my hand. The now bald, misshapen cactus stares up at me sideways, mocking me. How dare my mother, the one I haven't talked to in fifteen years, be the one to understand me? How could she have found a way to express the very feelings I haven't been able to put into words?

It's like there is a keg of gunpowder in my belly, dry harmless powder...until a fuse gets lit. Why are there so many fuses? And why can't I see them so I can step on them before they get lit? Why couldn't she have been this person when I was growing up?

Father Time comes around the corner, having to duck turn to come through the doorway into my room. "What's all the racket?" he asks in a whisper.

I put my hands behind my back to pull the thorns out of my palm. "What are you doing here?"

"I could ask you the same thing," he says.

"I'm looking for," I pause, not knowing how to finish the sentence. "Something," I mumble.

"Perfect. Because I have something to show you." He waves

his arm with the hourglass hanging off his wrist toward the living room.

I peek around the corner. I have to squint because the sliding glass doors have disappeared. The walls are back and there is very little light. The wood stove is back making those cracking sounds that always made me think it was going to blow up. And there is a bassinet in the living room with a baby wrapped in a pink blanket. A young girl, barely older than Sofia, is sitting as close to the basinet as she can, softly singing. "Is the baby...*me*?" I ask in awe.

He nods, his white beard bouncing up and down. "Yup. That's you."

"And the young girl? That's my mother?"

"Yes. She just brought you home from the hospital."

"How does a sixteen year old have a house?" I ask.

"Her mother gave it to her."

I snort. "That's great parenting, reward your pregnant sixteen year old by giving her a house."

"It's hardly a palace," he says. "And it wasn't a reward. She was only supposed to stay here until you were born. Her parents said she was at a boarding school in Europe."

"Mel? Queen of the Boot-Scootin-Boogie at a boarding school in Europe?" She looks so young, so much like Sofia, that I want to go in and hug her. She looks mesmerized, and terrified, as she stares at her baby. A child responsible for a baby.

"She was supposed to hide here until she gave birth." He adds, "And then she was supposed to give you away."

"What do you mean, give me away?"

"Your grandmother felt it brought shame upon a family to have a child out of wedlock."

"Well, her mother must have come around. No mother could leave her daughter, and her granddaughter, all alone."

"Do you ever remember meeting your grandmother?"

I turn away and stare at Father Time. "You're saying she

defied her mother to keep me? And that her mother completely cut her off for it?"

"Yes."

I turn back, staring at Amelia as hard as she is staring at her baby. Well, at me, I guess. "She chose me," I whisper in wonder. I always felt like she chose alcohol over me. But long before alcohol, she chose me. "She chose me," I repeat, the words so foreign on my tongue I can't comprehend them. "And her mother rejected her for it," I whisper. Then more comes to me and I can hardly stand. "Then I rejected her."

It was one thing to think of turning away from my mother when she was drinking. It's a whole other level of betrayal to imagine anyone else leaving this poor young girl alone with a baby. I have to fight the urge to go in, to hug her, to mother this young girl that is my mother.

"You had your reasons," Father time says in his deep voice. "Just like her mother probably thought giving you up was the best thing for her daughter."

"By threatening her? By giving her an ultimatum?"

"I don't show you this to make you doubt the past."

"Then why the hell would you show me this?" I whisper.

"Because there is no one single truth."

"Try telling that to Jack," I mumble.

"There's your truth. And her truth. And even her mother's, your grandmother's, truth. Jack is trying to help you recognize your own truth."

"And what are you trying to show me?"

"The whole truth."

My stomach revolts and I think I might be sick. "Why?"

"Don't you want to know the whole truth?"

I lean against the wall, closing my eyes because it's killing me to look at the past.

"You were marinated in rejection. And shame."

I slump further into the wall. "Is this supposed to make me feel better?" I whisper from the depths of my soul.

"Maybe not right now," he says gently. "But yes. Hopefully. Eventually." He puts his white glove under my chin and waits for me to open my eyes before he continues. "Someone once said, "Truth is like surgery. It hurts but it cures. Lies are like pain killers. Instant relief, but side effects, forever.""

I take a shuddering breath and he gives me a moment to absorb everything he is telling me.

"It's horrible that you were born in shame," he says. "But Jodi, you have to understand, it didn't start with you. It started with all the women in your family who came before you."

Chapter Twenty-Three

Jodi

It's been the longest week ever.

I feel unbalanced. My foundation is unsteady. Normal has never felt so appealing.

Standing at the gate at the airport, waiting for Sofia to come through customs, I can hardly wait to see her. I would have missed her any week she went away, but this week was anything but normal. I will take Sofia to the Italian place in the city for her favorite pizza. If she's not tired, we'll eat there. If she is worn out from the long flight from Japan, we'll take the food home and eat on the couch. A quiet night where I can hear all about her trip.

Sofia comes through the gate and throws herself into my arms, almost as if she missed me as much as I missed her. I hug her. This afternoon made me more aware than ever that time is fluid. And it never stops. Our thoughts may get stagnant and keep us stuck, but time marches on. With, or without us. And I'm going to soak the life out of every moment with her.

We get on the escalator to go to the baggage claim area. She's pressed tight to my side, talking fast, trying to tell me everything at once.

"Sofia! Surprise!" her friends scream from the bottom of the escalator, a bouquet of welcome home balloons floating over their heads.

She is now wrapped in their arms. Their youthful radiance glows around them like a iridescent bubble. My little girl isn't a little girl anymore. My legs almost buckle as I am overwhelmed with awe for the beautiful, tentative woman that she is becoming.

Meghan, a year older than Sofia, has her license and they want to take her out.

For a second, Sofia looks up at me, torn between her friends and me. My heart warms that I am part of her choice, but I don't need her to choose me. It isn't about her choosing me. It's about me letting her go.

We get her luggage off the carrousel. She gives me a kiss and a tight hug and then she's off with her friends. For one moment as she disappears around the corner, I feel bereft, her suitcase heavy on my arm. Then it hits me...if I'm not completely responsible for Sofia's happiness, then Amelia isn't responsible for my unhappiness.

I drop the suitcase and sit on it, fairly stunned by this revelation. Then another epiphany washes over me. If I can let go of who I love, with love, then surely I can let go of bad feelings.

I look around for Jack and Eartha, wishing I could share my revelations with them, but they're nowhere to be seen. I pick up Sofia's suitcase, which doesn't seem quite so heavy now, confident they both know.

I walk into my house. The house I've walked into so often that I don't even think about it. I can turn the lights on without looking because my hand automatically knows where the switches are. I can walk up and down stairs and although my mind couldn't tell you how many steps there are, my body knows. I can make it to the bathroom in the middle of the night without fully waking up.

I pour a glass of wine and take it upstairs. My clothes feel heavy and I shed them on the floor. I take a sip of wine and slip between the sheet. Then I lean over the bed and fish my cell phone out of my jean's pocket. When Bob answers, it sounds like I woke him up. I should have considered the time difference. "Did I wake you? I just wanted to let you know that Sofia got home safe and sound."

"I'm glad you called," he says. "It's a long flight, especially by yourself. Is she tired? Or wired?"

"I'm not sure. When I got to the airport, some of her friends surprised her. And I let her go with them."

"I'm sure that isn't what you planned for tonight," he says.

Lately, a lot of things have been happening around here that I haven't planned.

"I'm proud of you for letting her go," he says.

I am silent for a moment and let that sink in. "Thanks, Bob."

"Won't be long until she's off to college. We never really talk about what we're going to do when she goes to college. I feel like we know how to be Mom and Dad. But I sometimes wonder if we remember how to be husband and wife."

Wow! Has Bob found imaginary friends in Japan that are helping him see things that we've never talked about before. If you asked me if I have a good marriage I would have said yes without a single thought put into my answer. Or the question. Especially the question. Because then I would have to admit that I have no idea what a good marriage looks like. I was too busy figuring out what it meant to be a good mother.

"When I dropped Sofia off at the airport," he continues, "I picked up a book. *One Year to a New Relationship. Fifty-two weeks of fun and intimacy.*"

Bob? A self-help book? On relationships? "What's the first week?" I ask.

"It says to sit for three minutes and no talking. Just look into each other's eyes."

Gag! But I don't say anything.

"We obviously can't do that in different countries," he say. "So pick a number."

"Thirty-four."

I can hear him flipping through the book. "Phone sex," he says, sounding a lot more awake.

"You're making that up," I say.

"You picked it," he says. Long pause. "So, what are you wearing?"

Gag again. I pull the blankets tight up under my chin. I imagine what Eartha would be wearing when her lover calls her from another country. "I'm wearing a leopard corset."

He laughs.

"What's so funny?"

"You are not wearing a leopard corset."

Obviously I can't really argue. "Why don't you tell me what you'd like me to be wearing?" If he says a french maid's outfit, I'm not playing anymore.

"A smile."

I can't help myself. I do smile a little.

"It was your smile I fell in love with first," he says softly.

Even though he's told me this a hundred times, I still like hearing it.

"What about me?" he asks. "What do you want me to be wearing?"

I really don't know how to do this. We've barely been apart. I don't think we've ever done phone sex. I have no idea what to say. Cowboy? Indian Chief?

"I've got this," he says. "Close your eyes."

"Okay."

"Knock, knock."

I am not sure where he's going with this. Jokes are supposed to turn us on? "Who's there?"

"Pierre."

"Pierre who?"

"I'm your handy man. Your husband is away and he asked me to come over."

Oh My God! My husband of twenty years is going to start our foray into phone sex by imagining me have sex with a Frenchman?

"I am here to build you a very special project that your husband designed just for you."

"Okay," I say suspiciously.

"It's like a laundry shoot," he explains.

I thought I was going to be bad at phone sex. Bob is even worse.

"It goes from the attic right into the bathroom. It will automatically re-fill the toilet paper roll. And there's a truck coming later this afternoon with a life-time supply of toilet paper so that you will never run out again as long as you live."

He heard me. Honored my feelings. It doesn't change the fact that he will probably still forget to change it, but somehow knowing he listened, makes me feel better. I thought if my family loved me, they would do the things I asked. But these things aren't about me at all. My mother drank for her own reasons. Her drinking didn't mean she didn't love me, like I've been believing for years. Just because Bob doesn't notice the empty toilet paper doesn't mean he doesn't notice me.

Unraveling all this emotion is exhausting. I am emotionally spent. I snuggle under the covers. "Hey, Bob...?

"Yeah, honey?"

"I am wearing a smile."

Chapter Twenty-Four

Sofia

I lean against the wall near the ladies room, the base from the band making the wall shake. At least I tell myself it's the wall shaking, and not me. I can't believe they let me in to this dive bar. According to my fake ID, I am twenty-four years old. Meghan brought clothes for me to change into, including the best push-up bra I've ever seen. I'm waiting to get into the bathroom so I can take a picture of the label so I can order my own. I'm pretty sure I don't look twenty-four, but in this bra, at least my boobs do. And that's all the guy at the door looked at.

The beer is gross. I know I don't like beer cuz sometimes my Dad lets me have a sip of his. Then he laughs when I make a face worse than when I suck on a lemon. But since it's my first time in a bar, I didn't know what else to order.

I take a gulp of my beer and control my face, wishing my Dad was here to laugh at me. Then I look down at my impressive boobs and wish I wasn't such a loser. I wish I didn't need this stupid bra.

I watch my friends dancing. And flirting. And drinking. Looking so at ease, like they've been doing this all their lives. I know they've been here a couple of times without me, but still, they shouldn't look so comfortable.

Or I shouldn't feel so uncomfortable.

I am glad I am out with my friends. I wish I was home. I shift my weight from one foot to the other. The floor is so sticky I know every time I wear these shoes after tonight I'm going to feel stuck.

Lately, I can't make up my mind about anything. Seems no matter what I choose, it always feels wrong. Feels right, long enough for me to choose. And then when it's too late to change, it starts feeling wrong. So wrong it hurts. And it stays that way... until it's time to choose again.

Chapter Twenty-Five

Mel

I open the window behind my desk, inhaling the cool night air. I swear night air tastes darker than the bright air of day. A few papers blow off my desk but instead of closing the window, I put the extra paper in a drawer.

Just me, my pencil, and one blank page. That's all I need.

I bend my leg and lift my foot onto the chair. I shake off my slipper and roll up the bottom of my pajama pant. I pull my knee tight to my chest so I can see my one and only tattoo, on the side of my foot. *I am a spiritual being having a human experience.*

I got this tattoo the day I stopped drinking.

You'd think dropping my infant granddaughter, just hours after she was born, would be my rock bottom.

It wasn't.

Appallingly, I took that horrible, unforgivable behavior and turned it into permission to dive straight into the bottle. Arms tucked to my side, headfirst, falling as fast as possible, further into the bottle. And when Jodi stopped talking to me, if I'm completely honest, I felt like I was off the hook.

No one needed me. No one wanted me. The ultimate permission slip.

The next couple of years were a blur of drinking. And getting more and more sick, physically and emotionally, until I was just waiting to die. Living was simply a punishment.

And then one night, walking a couple miles home from work because I was too drunk to drive, I walked under the bridge I had walked through hundreds of times. Something tripped me. Probably my own feet. As I sat there, I couldn't think of a single reason to get up. So I just laid down. With no intention of ever getting up again. I was done. When the sun came up, the first rays of light splashed on the ground near my foot. And right there, in small letters, written in chalk...*I am a spiritual being having a human experience.*

The way that single ray of sun was shining specifically on that part of the cement felt like God was speaking directly to me. Daring me to acknowledge that I was more than a raging alcoholic. Maybe not much more, but still, more than nothing. That my sensitive soul scared the shit out of me. I had been drowning her for years with alcohol.

I got up. Walked home. And had that saying tattooed on my foot that very day. Each pin-prick of the needle felt like a wake up call. Painful and necessary at the same time.

And I haven't had a drink since.

But that was just the beginning because it turns out drinking wasn't my biggest problem. Being afraid of my feelings was underlying it all. Facing all my fears was the hardest thing I've ever done. Feelings are meant to move through us. No matter how hard and horrible, they will pass. Unless we don't let them. Drinking spared me from facing myself. It numbed me but it also kept all those feelings stuck inside. I was bottled up so tight, it was only a matter of time until it killed me. I was drowning inside of myself.

Which is why I draw. Drawing helps me understand my own feelings so I can process them and eventually let them go.

I open my phone and look at the picture of the mermaid I had drawn for Jodi this morning. A mermaid is the personification of my tattoo. My mantra. Half human and half magical. I start drawing.

I draw another mermaid. This one has three anchors tied around her waist, pulling her under, her little hands reaching for the surface, for the sun. I write on the anchors. *Be good. Be quiet. Behave.* All the things I thought I was supposed to be. And mostly wasn't.

Under the mermaid I write her caption. *Drowning...because she forgot she was a mermaid.*

That's how I felt that night under the bridge. Drowning because I denied my own messy, human, flawed life. Because I denied my magic. Not just my own, but the light within all of us. We are not all lucky enough to have someone show us our own beauty. Not everyone has a witness to their spirit. And sometimes it takes a very, very long time to become your own witness.

I put the drawing of the little mermaid on the corner of my desk, safe from the gentle breeze coming in the window, and grab another piece of paper, possessed with the urge to draw another mermaid. Addiction. Obsession. Two sides of the same coin. Addiction to drinking ruined my life. Obsession with drawing my feelings has saved me.

My next drawing has two mermaids. A mature mermaid with the words, 'Well-Behaved Woman,' tattooed on her own back is tattooing the same message on a younger mermaid. The younger mermaid looks a little stunned, her eyebrows furrowed, wondering what she's done wrong to deserve being labelled.

I look at the two mermaids and feel a weight in the bottom of my heart, wounds passed from one generation to another. If only I had known sooner that the stories we tell ourselves, the stories other people tell us about ourselves, can be changed. And I thank God, the Universe, and the Powers that Be, for this chance to change my story with Jodi.

I'm hopeful about Jodi and me and with hope, at least for me, comes a shitload of fear. Because it's not the big things that scare me. Have a baby by myself at sixteen? I can do that. Open a country bar when I know nothing about business, I can learn.

But when my Jodi got her period and I was supposed to be the one to teach her about being a woman, and being intimate with a man, my veins filled with ice. I froze in fear because I knew nothing about either. I was too afraid to learn, and even more afraid to try to teach her. So I drank.

And now I draw. Because I've learned that numbing cost me everything. So I'll hold on to the hope that Jodi and I can find our way back to each other. That she will find a way to forgive me and I will find a way to wait. If a mountain of fear is the cost of that hope, I'll pay it.

And keep drawing.

Chapter Twenty-Six

Jodi

My heart is ringing. I am sitting at a picnic bench in Sofia's favorite Italian restaurant, which is odd because they don't normally have picnic tables. The tables around ours are upside down but I'm too focused on the delicious chicken parmesan dinner in front of me, complete with the best garlic bread in the whole world, to notice. But I can't eat because my heart is ringing. Suddenly Bob is there and he takes a piece of my garlic bread. But he is in Japan so how can he be stealing my bread? And why doesn't someone answer my heart?

A couple of seconds later, I realize I have fallen asleep on top of the cordless phone.

Which also means there is no chicken dinner. Damn.

Is Bob calling back, ready to try another chapter in his new book? I press the button. "Hello?"

"Mrs. Devlin?"

"Yes."

"You have a daughter, Sofia?" the voice asks.

I am wide awake now. "Yes."

"This is Dartmouth Hospital. There's been an accident."

I rush into the emergency room. "My daughter's been in a car accident," I cry before I even reach the nurse at the desk.

"What's her name?"

"Sofia Devlin. Is she okay?"

"She's still unconscious. You can see her for two minutes. That's it. Then we're taking her for an MRI."

The nurse leads me to a blue curtain and slides it partially open. Sofia is lying on the stretcher. She looks like a doll that's been dropped on the ground, all disjointed and still. One arm is bent awkwardly at the elbow to accommodate an IV. There is a huge lump, swollen and discolored, on her forehead. Her jaw is slack and frozen, almost mid-scream. "I'm here, honey." I take Sofia's limp hand in my own. "Honey, open your eyes." Her blouse is ripped open and monitors are stuck on her chest. She looks cold and I want to climb on the bed and warm her with my body. "It's important that you open your eyes, honey. Just for a second. To let them know you're all right. For me, honey. Just for a second. Please, baby. Open your eyes."

The nurse touches my shoulders. "They're almost ready for her, Mrs. Devlin."

I try to back up. I really do. I know they are trained to help her more than I can. The nurse says I have to let her go but my DNA screams that life depends on me holding her close. I can no more let her go than I can make her open her eyes. "Sofia, please. One," I whisper. "Two...."

The nurse snakes her hands under my arms, hooking my shoulders and holding me tight against her own body. "Have you been able to reach her father?" she asks.

"I called him on my way here. He's in Japan. Trying to get a flight home."

She tries to lead me toward the desk but I don't want to leave Sofia.

She's asking me insurance questions that I can't answer because I can't think. I can't speak. I can't breathe. "Three," I say loudly to Sofia.

Her eyes are still closed. I would have hit the floor if the nurse wasn't still holding me up.

"Is there someone else we can call?" the nurse asks. "Someone who can be with you?"

"Mom," I sob. "I want my mother."

Chapter Twenty-Seven

Sofia

I struggle to open my eyes. I am so scared. And I'm floating above the room. I can see my own body lying broken on the bed. The fact that I can see my body, but I can't feel it, is freaking me out. I want nothing more than to open my eyes and tell my mother that I'm okay. Then I want her tell me that I'm okay, but no matter how much I can see from up here, I can't get my body to do anything but lie there and bleed.

Then she starts counting. "Great idea, Mom!" I say, surprised I can hear my voice, and somehow knowing no one else can hear me. Never once in my life have I let my mother get to the count of three. Even when I swore I wouldn't do what she asked, I couldn't help myself. I did whatever she wanted by the end of two, long before three. If nothing else, my body will automatically respond, bending to my mother's will.

One.

Nothing. I tried. But when I saw that my eyes didn't open, I still wasn't worried. I often let Mom get to two.

Two. Okay. Now I have to open my eyes.

Still nothing. More people come into the room. Then the nurse is wrestling my mother away from me. "Mom!" I scream, knowing no one can hear me.

I watch as they whisk my body away. Mom's broken, guttural, "Three," echoes in the hall behind me as the doors swing like a guillotine, cutting us off from each other.

Chapter Twenty-Eight

Mel

It's the middle of the night but I'm not tired. I have six little mermaid drawings swimming around on my desk. I close the window so I can move them around, switching the order. The faint idea of a story is floating around in my head as I move the drawings around. A theme is tickling at the edge of my consciousness. Maybe I'll go on-line and have these drawings put into a little hardcover book. I imagine giving it to Sofia at her high school graduation.

I know it's going to take a long time and a lot of trust, but in the middle of the night when everything is quiet and dark, I let myself dream.

I jump when the phone rings. One, because when I'm drawing I usually leave my phone in the other room and totally ignore it. And two, because a phone ringing this late is never good news.

I answer. Listen. Then drop the phone on my desk, scattering my drawings. Sofia's been in a car accident. Jodi is asking for me.

The very thing I've been praying for.

But not like this.

Please, God. Not like this!

Chapter Twenty-Nine

Jodi

My mother and the doctor come at me from different directions. Mom, wearing red sneakers, comes running in through the same doors I came in. The doctor in his blue scrubs comes toward me from the doors that they took Sofia through. My body is a lead weight, a magnet drawing them both toward me. "Is she okay?" I ask. "Can I see her?"

"They're taking her to the ICU," the doctor says in a calm voice. "As soon as she's settled into a room, I will take you to her."

"ICU?" Mom gets to me and holds me tight to her side.

He takes my arm and leads us to the faded plastic chairs. He can probably tell I'm ready to sprint out of this waiting room to wherever they have her hidden in the bowels of the hospital.

"We've put her in a medicated coma," he explains.

Mom holds my hand. A medicated coma? Medicated or not, he's telling me that my baby is in a coma.

He keeps talking and I can tell he's trying to talk in simple terms but all I want to do is get to Sofia.

The longer the doctor talks, the harder I squeeze my mother's hand. If he keeps talking I'm afraid I will break her fingers, but I can't stop. And she doesn't ask me to.

Chapter Thirty

Sofia

Looking down at my body, bruised and bleeding and so still, creeps me out. I don't look old enough to have spent the night in a bar. Drinking. I didn't even really want to be there but there was no way I was admitting that to my friends. So I went along with everything.

Then the more I drank, the less I worried. Drank until I was barely thinking. So when some guy offered me a ride home, I said yes. Even though I didn't know him. Didn't know if he'd been drinking. Was he somewhere in this hospital? I vaguely remember hearing the ambulance guy saying the driver was fine, too drunk to notice hitting a tree. And that he was wearing his seatbelt.

I also heard them say I wasn't wearing mine.

I am in so much trouble. Might as well tell them not to worry about me because my mother is going to kill me. I start pacing, floating from one side of the room to another. Does Mom know about the fake ID? She probably knows about the guy in the car, too. And they're probably testing my blood so she'll know I'd been drinking.

Suddenly, a bunch of machines start beeping and I hear someone say, "Her heart rate is rising!"

I look down and see them cut my state-of-the-art bra

off. I'm annoyed, and embarrassed, at the same time. Still floating on the ceiling, I wish I could cover myself up but there are so many people and machines around my body that there isn't room.

I float high up in the corner, as far away from everything as I can get.

"I find it's best if you don't watch."

I feel like those words are meant for me. Someone can see me? I stare down at all the doctors and nurses, trying to find the one that might be talking to me. Might be able to see me.

"I'm right here," the same voice says, and I look up. There, floating near the ceiling, just like me, is an old woman.

"Don't watch," she says. "It's not you anyway."

"Sure looks like me," I say, but take her advice anyway and stop watching them try to fix me.

"Well, it is you. But it's only part of you," she says.

She pulls me on her lap and, like a child, I let her. "You feel almost as good as my Mom," I say, more tired than I have ever been in my life. "You kinda remind me of her."

"That's the nicest compliment you could give me," she says softly in my ear.

"I want to go back," I mumble, my eyes so heavy I think my head might literally fall off my neck.

She rests my head on her shoulder. "That's not up to me."

"Then who is it up to?" I ask, shivering. It's so cold in here.

She shrugs, her luminous shoulder making the air around her shimmer with iridescent waves of energy. "Rest, baby girl," she says, somehow warming me from inside. "Just rest."

And I do.

Chapter Thirty-One

Jodi

There is an eerie quiet in the Intensive Care Unit. The heart monitor beeps a steady rhythm but I don't need that to know Sofia's heart is beating because I am more connected to her than any monitor. My heart is beating, which means hers is too, because I honestly believe if hers stops, mine will too.

Bob won't get here until tomorrow afternoon. A flight that went through Florida would have gotten him here in the early morning but there was a hurricane warning that could have delayed his flight, so we agreed he should take the later flight that connected through New York. We've been here for hours, Sofia, me, and my mother. Sofia is sleeping. Resting. Recovering. Those are the only words I will allow myself to acknowledge. We will just stay here, in this room, until Sofia is fine. The only thing we have to do right now is wait. Wait for Sofia to be fine.

Mom is sitting in a chair pulled up to the other side of Sofia's bed. Sofia's hand on that side has an IV in the back of her hand so Mom is gently holding Sofia's forearm. The veins on the back of my Mom's hand have always been prominent. I have a vague memory of tracing her veins when I was little as if they were a treasure map. Her thinner skin is a beautiful contrast against Sofia's firm skin. Their pale skin, the same color, a beautiful contrast of youth and maturity.

Fifteen years ago it was me in the hospital bed after having given birth to Sofia. I can see my Mom waltzing into the room like it was a party. I can see her holding my baby, can feel the contraction in my own body as if I knew something bad was going to happen. Mom was saying something about showing Sofia the sun and started walking toward the window. She tripped over my suitcase. Thank God Bob was paying as much attention as I was. He caught Mom's arm and kept them both from falling. And then, he took Sofia from her. Seeing the moment again in my memory, I admit it was not quite as bad as I've made it out to be. Sofia didn't free-fall for ten thousand feet. Amelia stumbled and Bob caught them.

But I was already pissed at her because I had called her the night before when I went into labor, and of course she hadn't answered. Sofia was twelve hours old before Bob could finally reach her. And she took her sweet time getting there. Hopefully trying to sober up from the night before, but more likely having another drink.

A feeling of helplessness snakes through my bloodstream, menacing, as Sofia's doctor comes around the corner. My adrenaline kicks in. I stand beside Sofia's bed. Fight or flight. If he has good news, he can stay. Because he is not welcome in this room with any other kind.

"We go in order of concern," he says. "First things first. We have to get the swelling on her brain down. Second, she had very serious damage to one kidney. Which in and of itself, isn't too big a deal because we can always take it out if it doesn't heal properly."

His medical jargon is so confusing. Thing that sounds terrible, medicated comas and possible kidney removal are presented as good things. "And she'll be fine with only one kidney?" I ask.

"Yes. We hope we don't have to remove it but it's last resort option. The problem is, her other kidney is also showing signs of distress. It's not something we have to worry about just yet. The medication may fix one, or if we're really lucky, both. But we like to be prepared for the worst, so we need you to go downstairs to the lab to be tested to see if you're a match."

This is more than I can bear. But I won't cry in front of Sofia. "I don't want to leave her."

My Mom comes over to my side of Sofia's bed. "I will be right here. I will guard her with my life," Mom says. "You go. And when you come back, they can test me."

I lean over Sofia and kiss her forehead. "I'll be right back," I say, afraid to leave. I turn around at the door. "Mom, I couldn't do this without you."

"You could, but you don't have to." She smiles. "I won't let you down this time," she promises.

I believe her.

Chapter Thirty-Two

Mel

Jodi came back from the test, obviously disappointed. She isn't a match. Somehow she feels she has betrayed Sofia by not having the right blood type.

I remind her that we don't want to go that route anyway. And that Bob can be checked tomorrow.

Then I go down and get tested. My initial test shows I am a perfect match.

I came back to the room. Sofia looks like a sleeping Princess, waiting for her hero.

Or, in this case, her heroine.

"Great news," I say. "I'm a match."

Jodi's face lights up. Then she realizes if she is happy I am a match, that means she's acknowledging her child might need it. Her face goes blank again. Exhaustion. Denial. Avoidance.

"We'll count on Murphy's Law. Since we have a match, she won't need it." Then I tell her since we are obviously spending the night, I will go and get her some clean clothes. Her phone charger. A toothbrush and toothpaste. I do the errands as quickly as I can because I have one more thing I need to do before I can go back.

For once, I don't take a deep breath when they buzz the door to the nursing home. Why bother? I bring the baby dolls that were in my trunk to the nurses station.

"Miss Dorothy is having a good day," the nurse tells me.

I hand her the bag. "I might have to go away for a while, so I've ordered a few more dolls to be delivered in Miss Dorothy's name. Can you keep them hidden somewhere so you can replace them in case she loses one and I'm not here to do it?"

I can see her wondering where is she going to store ten dolls. Then I see her remembering the impressive tantrum Miss Dorothy throws when she can't find her baby. She takes the bag and smiles. "I hope you're going somewhere good."

I swallow and force a smile in return. "Me, too."

I go into the library and see Miss Dorothy, her wheelchair right next to the grand piano. I'm surprised she is there since it's not my usual day. Miss Dorothy is brushing her dolls hair and smiles brightly when she sees me. I don't have any small talk in me today so I simply sit on the wooden bench and flex my fingers. I sink into this moment and let everything else disappear as my fingers glide across the keys, the soft notes of her favorite song filling the room.

I finish the song and turn on the bench. "I'm might have to go away for a while," I say.

"Why are you going away?" she asks, her face getting that dark, disappointed look I remember all too well. "You going to jail?"

"No, I'm not going to jail." I get up and pace, trying not to be annoyed. But I'm annoyed as hell anyway. "Why do you always think the worst of me?" I mumble, not expecting her to answer me.

"I'm sorry, Amelia. I shouldn't."

I turn around. Dorothy never calls me by my name. I tell myself not to get excited. It doesn't mean anything. I've been volunteering here for years. Dorothy had heard the nurses and patients say my name a hundred times.

Then again, they always call me Mel. "You shouldn't what?" I ask slowly, sitting back down on the bench and facing her.

"Think the worst," she says. "You've been a good daughter."

I freeze. Then lean closer. I look deep into Dorothy's milky eyes. "Mom?" I whisper.

She pats her doll with one hand and strokes the side of my face with her other. "Amelia Jayne,"

Oh my God! "Mom?"

"Amelia Jayne," she says, her voice thready from lack of use. "I'm sorry."

I sit shock still, stunned. Afraid if I move this moment might not be happenning. Miss Dorothy...*my mother*...hasn't strung sensible words together in years.

"I should never have stopped seeing you." She starts to reach for my hand but slowly pulls hers back when I don't move. "In my day," she says, "if you got pregnant before you were married, you had to give the baby away."

I'm struggling to comprehend what she's saying.

"I thought it was the only choice. The best thing for you."

"I could only come back into your life when you forgot me."

"I never forgot you. Never. Ever. You remember the first time you came here?" she asks.

"Yes. They said I had to sign some papers since I was your only living relative."

"I moved myself here. At that time, I could still sign for myself. I had them call you so you would come. I wanted to ask for your forgiveness. Had planned everything I would say. How I thought it was my only choice. Your only choice."

My chest is heavy with the weight of unsaid words. "You made me choose between my baby and my mother."

"Worst thing I ever did," she says.

"So why didn't you tell me that day?"

"I was afraid. I didn't know how to ask. I didn't deserve to be forgiven."

"So you asked me to play," I say, remembering that day. I remember being grateful to the disease that made her forget me because it let us be together again.

"I did. And every time you came back, I swore that was going to be the time I asked for forgiveness. But I was so afraid. And then words got harder. And I started forgetting what it was I wanted to say. I just knew when you walked in, I'd see your red shoes, and my day got brighter."

"I felt guilty sometimes for being grateful for this disease that let me be your daughter again."

"I knew you were my daughter. Every single time. What I didn't know was how to ask you to forgive me." She picks her baby doll up off her lap and gently lifts the dolls dress. My name, Amelia Jayne, is embroidered on the dolls chest with a chain link stitch sewn in the shape of a heart around my name. "I would hide my doll when I was afraid you weren't coming back," she says softly.

"But, Mom, I always came back."

She takes a hovering breath, like she's been crying for years. "So sorry," she says, her spine caving in, making her even smaller in the wheelchair. She clutches her baby doll in her frail hands and shakes it. "Baby," she says, her voice weak. “Find the babies.”

I lean forward, reaching for her. She drops the doll on her lap, holding my hands tightly. The same hands Jodi held hours ago. She’s drifting away from me. I know it’s seconds before she will be unreachable again. I can see her struggling to stay with me, to hold on to the connections in her brain while the insidious disease is trying to pull us apart. I squeeze her hand, trying to help her stay with me. She’s struggles to say something, struggling to get the words from her heart, into her vocal chords, and to me. “I. Love. You,” she manages to say.

Tears fall from my eyes as words fall from my lips. “I love you, Mom!” I say loudly, penetrating the distance between us. Words I didn’t know I needed to say. Didn’t know were stuck in my heart until they came out. “I love you, too, Mom,” I whisper again.

The blankness comes over her face but instead of the empty, vacant stare, I swear she looks more peaceful than I ever remember seeing her. I am grateful in every cell of my being that if these are the last words that my mother and I are ever able to say to each other, they are words of forgiveness and love.

Chapter Thirty-Three

Sofia

I'm bored. I tried leaving the room but when I did, something strange happened. It's like the further I got away from my body, the more I disappeared. So I stay in the room. And feel guilty that my Mom is hurting. And I'm wondering who this other woman is who keeps rubbing Mom's back. She keeps telling her I'm going to be fine. She even got my mother to eat some breakfast this morning. And that made me wonder why I'm not hungry.

I feel like I'm playing ping-pong by myself. Guilty. Bored. Guilty. Bored.

So I'm thrilled when the old lady from the Titanic—that's how I'm thinking of her since she never told me her name —comes floating into my room. I want to ask her what she's doing here. Is she in a hospital bed somewhere? A part of me wonders if she is already dead? But it seems like a rude question and I'm already in enough trouble, so instead I ask, "Do you know who that is that's with my mother?"

"I do," she says, looking down at them both.

"She seems nice. She really likes my Mom."

"Yes. She does." She sighs. "That's your grandmother."

"It can't be. My grandmother did something so awful

that my mother doesn't talk to her. And she doesn't talk about her either."

"She had some problems. She visited your mother in this very hospital when you were born. She was drunk. And she dropped you. If your father hadn't caught you, well, never mind, he did. But your mother stopped talking to her after that."

I watch this woman who does look like Mom. She moves her hands like my Mom. Rubs my Mom's back just like my Mom rubs my back. I don't know this woman, but it's like I know her anyway. "My grandmother," I say out loud, trying the words on. I watch them sit, one on each side of my bed, quietly together. "Do you think they missed each other?" I ask softly.

"I certainly do," she answers softly.

"I can't imagine not talking to my Mom ever again."

"At the time, your mother thought there was only one choice. And, I suppose, in some ways there was. She had to make the choice that would keep her baby safe. Keep you safe."

I looked at the old lady. Was she criticizing my Mom? I jump to her defense. "Isn't that what any mother would do?"

"Sometimes we do things, thinking it's the right choice, and it's only later that we realize we made a huge mistake." She watches my Mom, and my grandmother—that word feels funny on my tongue—like she's studying a science experiment. Or aliens. Or something she wants to eat. I don't like it. They are my family, not hers.

Suddenly the idea of never seeing my Mom again seems way too real. "I don't want you! I don't want a grandmother!" I shout. "I just want my Mom!" I cry.

"Everything in my being wants to reunite you with your mother. I'm here so you won't be scared."

"Well, it's not working. I'm scared as shit!"

"Your family was broken a long time ago. And that's why we are here. To put it back together again."

"So let me go back. Please, let me go back to my mother. She can't lose me. And please...I can't never see my Mom again."

"I'm trying, Sofia. I'm really trying."

Chapter Thirty-Four

Jodi

One minute things are fine.

The next second the beat on the heart monitor goes a little faster. Five seconds later it gets louder. Ten seconds later an alarm goes off. Within fifteen seconds, people are rushing into Sofia's room. They push me aside and I have to let go of Sofia's hand. I scramble to the head of the bed, squeezing myself against the wall, my hand holding the top of Sofia's head. Her baby fine hair wraps itself around my fingers.

More people come running into the room. The chaos in the air is choking me. "No!" I cry. "Please, no!" I don't even know who I'm talking to. Just no. No. No!

They rip the heart monitor off her chest. I hear them unlock the brake on Sofia's bed. They're getting ready to take her. Before I can stop them, before I can say I love you, say something, anything, they take her away.

The room shimmers through my tears. Someone shuts the alarm off. No more beat.

Chapter Thirty-Five

Mel

I half drag, half carry Jodi to the hospital chapel. I hold her up with one arm and open the heavy wooden door with the other. "Mom," she's crying into my ear, "I don't think I can live without her."

There are only five pews. We stumble to the front and Jodi drops onto the bench with a loud crash. I hit my knees and start praying to the statue of Mother Mary. "One mother to another," I say, "you can't take her child from her. I'm telling you, Mary, I will take on God himself because... You. Can't. Have. Sofia!"

Jodi slides off the bench onto her knees beside me. Her breathing is so quick and shallow I'm afraid she is going to pass out. We are pressed together, side by side, literally joined at the hip. I match my breathing to hers, longer breath in, longer breath out, to get her to slow down her own breathing. Once she is a bit calmer, I wrestle us back onto the bench. We could be here a while. "I'm going to let the nurse know where we are,"

Jodi simply nods, so still she's practically a statue herself.

In the hall I bump into the doctor as he's racing by.

"We'll be in the chapel when you need to find us," I say, keeping up with him as he races to the elevator.

"I'll have the nurse let you know what's going on as soon as I know." He presses the elevator button even though he's already pressed it twice. "I heard you telling Jodi you're a match —"

I interrupt him. "I am. It's the truth."

"But it's only part of the truth." He starts speaking slowly as if he's talking to a child. But I'm not a child. I'm a Mama Bear.

"You only have one kidney yourself," he says.

"That is my patient information. You can't disclose it."

He stares at me like he's trying to decide if I actually understand what he's saying. "That means you can't donate the only one you have."

I nod so that he knows I understand.

Waiting for the elevator, he says, "You're not doing her any favors by not telling her the truth."

"Look, Doc. You said yourself it's just a precaution. So she doesn't need to worry about that yet."

"Yet," he emphasizes. "I'm telling her she shouldn't worry yet."

"You think right now she can tell the difference?" I ask.

He shakes his head right as the elevator dings. "Let's hope her father gets here in time and that he is a match." He squeezes through the doors before they even fully open and starts pressing the button. "We'll know a lot more in the next twelve hours."

I wait for the door to close and pull my phone out of my back pocket. I dial Jake's number by habit. "I need a favor," I say as soon as he picks up.

"What can I do for you?" he asks. "And I sure hope it involves nudity again."

I swallow. "My granddaughter has been in a car accident."

"Is she okay?"

"If I have anything to say about it, she is."

"Then it's a done deal," he says. "She's going to be fine."

His confidence in me is the exact encouragement I need. "She might need a kidney. The good news is I'm a match. Her mother isn't a match and her father is flying back from Japan. He might be a match but we don't know if he'll get here in time."

"Then she's one lucky granddaughter to be getting yours."

"I absolutely will give her mine. Without a moment's hesitation. The problem is I only have one kidney." There is a long silence. I don't fill it. I don't need to because I know he understands what I'm saying.

"Then how can you...?"

I don't say anything.

"Mel, you can't..."

"I can. And I will," I say with absolute conviction. "We're hoping the medicine will work. There's a chance her father could be a match. And that he'll get here in time."

"That's a lot of ifs. A lot of chances," he says. "A lot of hope."

Hope and I have a funny relationship. I love her, and I hate her, at the same time. Because I don't want to die. Not now. "I'm sure it won't come to that," I say, trying to sound positive.

"Mel, I'm serious. We need to find every other single option that is out there." His breath is ragged. "I don't want to lose you," he says softly. "I love you. I haven't said it because I know you don't want to hear it, but if we're gonna have this conversation, I'm gonna say it."

Tears stream down my face. All those years of not caring if I lived or died. All those years being alone. I drank alone. I sobered up alone. I've never been brave enough to try living a life with love. But now I'm sober and I have Jodi. And Sofia. And Jake. A life filled with love. Now, when it might be too late.

"I love you, too, Jake," I whisper into the phone. "But if Sofia needs me, if it comes to that, I need to make sure someone finds me." I take a deep breath. "Will you be my someone?"

I hear him swallow. "I already am, baby. I am your someone."

I take a moment and hold those words in my heart. Then I need to be sure he understands. "I need you to find me. With enough time to save Sofia. But not enough time to save me."

"I know what you're asking. And if it comes to that, I will do a lot more than find you," he says, his voice deep and full of promise. "I will be with you. Whatever you need."

For the first time, there is no fear battling for space in my heart with hope. Simply because there is just too much love. My love for Jodi, my only child. For Sofia, her only child and my only grandchild. My love for Jake.

No matter what happens, I have found the courage to hope.

Chapter Thirty-Six

Jodi

It is one month after the accident. Thirty days. Seven hundred and twenty hours.

I am walking up the path at the Fox Hill Cemetery. Hundreds of headstones with words chiseled in stone float in front of my eyes. Loving mother. Beloved daughter. So many fathers and sons. Sisters and brothers. I feel the ghosts of other families who have lost someone and walked this same path. The almost violent ride of emotions between grief and gratitude is making me dizzy. I hold on tighter to Bob, trying not to crush the three white roses he's holding. Off to my right, standing by a huge tree, I see Eartha and Jack. I nod my head to acknowledge them. Eartha lifts her hand, her white handkerchief a stark contrast to her black gloves. She lifts the black netting that folds from the edge of her hat, covering her face, to wipe her tears. Jack looks somber in his black suit.

I pull Sofia tight to my side. Gratitude so profound swells within my body. She's been out of the hospital for a couple of weeks. The doctor said she was very lucky there was no permanent damage. And that her recovery was almost a miracle.

It's been hard to let her out of my sight and it seems she feels the same way. I know in time we will both get more comfortable being away from each other, but for now, we are almost always touching in some little way. Grounding us. Somehow the accident has changed her. Given her the confidence to be herself. She seems more comfortable in her own skin than she has in a very long time.

In honor of my mother we are both wearing red shoes. I have flat, red ballet shoes on and Sofia has sequined red Converse. Certainly not appropriate funeral footwear, but I've stopped thinking of how things should be. I know my mother will appreciate the gesture. Looking at Sofia in her sparkling sneakers, this is a perfect example of how she's changed. Before the accident, Sofia would have scoffed at the idea of wearing red shoes.

Jack waves to get my attention. He pulls up the bottom of his pant leg to show me his red, polka dotted sox. From the grin on his face, I can tell he's wearing matching boxer briefs but Eartha holds his hand, just in case he's tempted to show me those, too. Jack reminds me a bit of my mother. Packaged very differently, but willing to put their hearts out in the world, despite knowing it will be broken. I plan to honor them both by being braver with my own heart.

Chapter Thirty-Seven

Mel

The graveyard is so beautiful. No where else in the city has this many glorious trees and the birds seem to be singing the songs of angels. The graveyard teeming with life seems like an affront to grieving families. Maybe they don't notice but it's all I can see.

The beauty in the world.

I watch my daughter and my granddaughter come up the path with Bob. Red shoes, different but the same, tangible proof that we belong together. A family.

A week ago, when the nurse told me my mother didn't have much time left, I told Jodi. I didn't think she would want to meet the woman who had tried to make me give her away, but I am done with secrets. Done with thinking we know better and should spare people difficult choices. It was up to Jodi whether she wanted to take this last chance to meet her grandmother.

She said yes.

My mother wasn't able to speak, but the minute she saw us walking in to her room together, her eyes lit up. Jodi pulled a chair right in front of Mom's wheelchair. They held hands and stared into each other's eyes. Two women, one before me and one after me, brave, saying more with no words than many people say in a lifetime.

When Jodi showed her a picture of Sofia, she took the photo out of Jodi's hand and stared at it. A single tear rolled down my mother's cheek. She took her baby doll off her lap and gave it to Jodi. She folded her hands around the photo of Sofia and held it close to her chest. She wasn't just showing Jodi her baby doll. She was trading it for the picture.

Introducing my daughter to my mother was the final stitch in mending my heart that had torn apart all those years ago. The fact that Jodi was forty and my mother was almost ninety didn't matter.

A few days later, my mother died peacefully in her sleep.

Sofia tugged on my arm. "Nan...."

Hearing Sofia call me that is so precious it breaks my heart every time. Thankfully, I have learned that a broken heart is the way more light gets in.

"That's her," she says, pointing to the picture on the casket.

"Who?" Jodi and I ask at the same time.

"The woman I told you about," she says, a big smile on her face. "The one who kept me company in the hospital."

Chapter Thirty-Eight

Dorothy

If I had known my funeral would be one of the proudest moments in my life, I might have died sooner.

I see Bob hand a single white rose to each of my girls. My precious daughter, Amelia, Jodi, my granddaughter, and Sofia, my great-granddaughter. Arms entwined, they step forward and lay the trio of roses on my gleaming casket.

Three generations of women gathered here, at my side, to wish me safe travels. More than I deserved, more than I could have ever hoped for. They seem to think this is goodbye. Silly girls. Now that we're back together, they're crazy if they think I'm ever really leaving them.

Broken families can heal. Generational pathology, while it runs deep, doesn't have to drown everyone. Like a river, it can change course. It takes a lot of hard work, and the commitment of a lifetime, but it can be done. I inherited and passed down wounds from generations of women, too many to count. For that, I am eternally sorry. In the end though, I helped interrupt the family pattern of abandonment, and for that, I am eternally grateful.

One day soon, when Amelia is drawing at her desk,

the mailman will deliver a package from the nursing home. When I first moved in, when I still had my wits with me, they assigned me a locker in the back where I could put my valuables. Things I didn't want to get lost. I put three very special packages in there, to be mailed when I died. Mel will get one of the first baby dolls she brought me. I will be in the breeze that lifts the dress so Mel can see the heart I carefully embroidered in red thread, with her name stitched inside of it. Just one more reminder that I never forgot her. That I never will.

Mel will see the imperfect thread dangling from the bottom of the otherwise perfectly stitched heart. I know that hanging thread will bother her. She always was a curious little girl and she won't be able to help herself. She will pull on it. It's just who she is. I wish I could have always appreciated her for who she is.

By pulling on it, she will find the gift I left inside. The name of the bank and the account number that I left for her. A legacy I am proud to leave for my family. Of course, I also left instructions with my lawyer, just in case she doesn't find the dangling thread. But I know my daughter. She will find it first.

She will call Jodi, who will also have a package from the mailman of her own doll that will have her name lovingly stitched within the heart. And, of course, another one for Sofia.

I know they will spend hours around Jodi's kitchen table discussing what to do with the money I left them. Save it. Invest it. Combine it all for Sofia's college, even though her own account is enough for that. They will take a long time, not because they can't agree. And not even because they care that much about the money. It's the together they are all craving from years of thirsting for family.

Seeing my girls together, I am proud to say we have closed the circle. Broken the cycle. The sun shimmers on a particular shade of red that runs through all their hair. Same as mine. That intangible thread of DNA, once tangled and twisted, is now beautifully woven through all our hearts, bonding us forever.

I will keep an eye on my girls for the rest of their lives.

I will be in the ray of sun that streams in the church window when Mel marries Jake.

I will be the dream Jodi has that she can't quite remember but has her smiling throughout the day.

I will be the whisper of courage, or caution, whichever is needed, as Sofia continues to grow into the woman we are all so proud of.

And I am already planting seeds that Jayne is a lovely name for someday, far in the future, when Sofia will give birth to a daughter. The first girl in our family to have the privilege of being adored by generations of women.

That little Jayne, armed with the feminine wisdom of these incredible women, will be the beginning of a whole new story for our family. Many years from now, she will sit on her great-grandmother's lap. Mel, her fingers stiff with age, will draw her final mermaid for her beloved little Jayne. This time, the young mermaid who was being tattooed with the words "Well-Behaved Woman," will have a sea sponge tied to a stick and will be washing the family legacy off her back.

With a mischievous look in her eye and her eyebrow tipped in a daring wink, her caption will be, Well-Behaved Woman...Wanna Bet!

The End...

and The Beginning.

WELL
BEHAVED
WOMAN
wanna bet?
LifePonderings

Dear Reader,

Just like Mel, I use art to express things that I cannot put into words. All those little beings that Mel made. . . the onion girl who can't stop crying, the cactus girl who just wants a hug, the girl being mummified by her To Do list, came straight from my heart and hands.

The Mermaid musings, also from the depth of my heart, were a siren song leading this story home.

If they speak to you, or for you, you can find them at DeborahMonk.com.

Deborah Monk
July 2018

About the Author

Deborah was born to be a writer but took a detour of passion as a professional ballroom dancer. While she traveled the world on the competitive circuit, she never stopped her pen from dancing across the page knowing, in time, she would return to her first dream. Deborah's dance, her written words, and her art all have the underlying message of empowering women through self-discovery.

She is the host of a weekly podcast, The Writer's Block Podcast NH. She lives in New Hampshire with her husband and has raised an incredible, world-traveling daughter.

A self-proclaimed Life Ponderer, you can find her books and her art at DeborahMonk.com

Made in the USA
San Bernardino, CA
26 October 2018